June Caravel

Pregnant at any price!

Novel

FROM THE SAME AUTHOR…

Other books by the same author are about to come out or have already been released...

To discover the entire universe of June Caravel, go to http://www.junecaravel.com.

You will receive free excerpts and know before everybody when the next books will be released by subscribing to the newsletter.

Already released:

—— The curse of holiday romance, 2020

—— Pregnant at any price!, 2021

To be released:

—— Wild Card, 2022

© June Caravel 2021
www.junecaravel.com

Illustration: Félix Rousseau

Edition: BoD - Books on Demand,
12/14 Champs-Élysées roundabout, 75008 Paris
Printing: BoD - Books on Demand, Norderstedt, Germany
ISBN : 978-2-322399-15-4
Registration of copyright: November 2021

Dépôt légal : Novembre 2021

All rights reserved for all countries

FIRST CHAPTER
THE CLOCK IS TICKING

I don't think I ever really paid attention to that well-known biological clock until I was jilted by my boyfriend at 31. And for good reason! I had been living with him for more than two years and I was convinced he was the man of my life and the father of my future children.

But when he told me at 11.38am that morning: "There's no good moment to tell you this so I'll just say it: I'm leaving you."

My first reaction was: "Is this a joke?"

My second was: "How can you do this to me?"

And my last was: "So you'll never be the father of my children?"

And there it was! My biological clock had just started ticking ever so loudly!

In this day and age though, at thirty you're still considered "young". I have plenty of girlfriends who were still childless at that age. However when you don't have the guy anymore, being 31 is the beginning of the end, or rather, the start of the countdown.

Because not only are you back in the "singles" category, an enchanting world you had left with joy to finally settle down, but now you have to find the guy that won't just see you as the next prey for a one-night-stand but rather as for keeps. Knowing that all the right guys are already taken and that if they're not it's either because:

1. They still want to take advantage of their youth, that

is to say screw anything that moves.

2. They have a panic fear of commitment, which is almost equal to the first category.

3. They are so ugly, dumb or a mix of both, that no one wants them.

4. They are gay.

So we're in deep shit, us girls! And then, at that very moment, you happen to read an article while waiting at the dentist's that says you've by-passed your fertility peak by at least six years! That's right, silly cow, the best age to make babies is from age 15 to 25! From 25 onwards, fertility lowers every year asymptotically (don't ask me what it means, I gave up on maths a long time ago). And the risk of conceiving a child with Down's syndrome increases every year exponentially (there again, can't help with the maths). And at 40, unless there's a miracle, you're fit for the scrap-heap. Anyway who would have enough energy to have a child at 40?

At this stage, you're in total panic. You always thought you would have children in your early thirties. But you have to face it: you don't have the guy. And even if you had him, unless you run into a man who only dreams of one thing, having kids–that is to say something like 0,001% of the male population?–Well, you can forget about having children around 30…

That's when you register reluctantly on a dating website (where you had sworn never to go again, since you had tested it and met a crazy snorer last time) and that you start talking to men who only visibly want to fuck with you (our categories 1 and 2 above) or the ugly or dumb or both (category 3 above).

A week later, you cancel your account, tired of hearing

every time you log on a laconic: "Hey, you're hot, wanna have a drink?" from a 50 year old man with a beer belly that goes up to his chin (a fifth category you hadn't experienced until then).

That's when you read yet another article at your dentist's (unfortunately the filling needed more work) that says that thanks to a revolutionary technique your eggs can be extracted and stored in a sort of freezer, in case you don't find the right guy straight away. The only drawback is that the operation costs three thousand euros. And another three hundred euros a year to preserve them.

Your friends–in a relationship–say: "Don't worry, you have all the time in the world, you're only thirty-one, you will find someone else."

Except years go by, men too and you still can't find the one. You forgot about the opportunity to deep freeze your eggs because you were optimistic and you thought you were going to find someone… Ah, hope! It's true, your girlfriends keep saying: "You're neither ugly nor stupid, you make a good living, you will find him… Plus it costs a fortune and worst-case scenario, you will take one on AdoptAGuy or Tinder, you can get pregnant behind his back, and worst case scenario, you can always become a single mum…"

OK, but there's AIDS and you don't want to have unsafe sex with the first guy you meet. And most of all, you don't want to have a baby without a father!

I remember a conversation I recently had with my best friend, Luana, who had found her Prince Charming after we came back from Mexico:

"Julia, you're always looking for cute men, who cheat or leave you in the end. Don't you want to lower your expectations and take a man who will be a little less good-looking but nice, respectful and serious?

"I went out with men like that."

"And what happened?"

"I was the one who left them."

Lowering my expectations... It was like giving me the choice between eating celery–a good guy but not really cute–and a slice of my favourite cake–a good and really handsome guy.

Frankly, who chooses celery? But at the same time, I had to admit my strategy up until then hadn't worked and I was ready to do anything to find the man of my dreams and have children as soon as possible. Maybe I was condemned to eat celery my entire life while watching others stuff their faces with my favourite chocolate cake. The sort of diet which could only end up going off the rails.

I was now 33 and kept thinking about all this–literally obsessed with my biological clock–when I decided to go and visit my best friend for a week-end at Le Tréport in Normandy.

CHAPTER 2
ONE GLASS TOO MANY

I am not one of those girls who remain friends with their exes. To me a male friend is something fishy. There's always–as far as I'm concerned–something sexually implied in any male-female relationship.

I had always been attracted to my best friend, John. But here's the thing: he's gay and he's never been tempted to try it with a girl, so it was the only masculine friendship I had allowed myself.

John has been living for five years with Matthias and I do get along very well with both of them. So when they asked me to round for a week-end in their Normandy cottage, I was glad about the change of air.

I think I have never admitted to John that I had always been attracted to him. What would it have changed anyway? I wasn't even fuckable for him. It had always intrigued me that he was never attracted to the opposite sex. As far as I'm concerned, I had had a moment of doubt at about 17, when I kissed the best friend of my then boyfriend in a sort of improvised threesome. I had thought kissing a girl was ok–it was a bit like kissing a man– but the rest was really too weird!

At least I was sure of something: I wasn't a lesbian. As a result, I couldn't understand why John didn't even try, not even to know if he was bisexual.

The three of us were sitting on the sofa in their cottage at Le Tréport talking about my latest short-lived conquests in categories 1 and 2, laughing rather than crying about it, when all of a sudden John said:

"In the end, I kind of would have wanted to see what it's like with a girl…"

Matthias opened his eyes wide and said to John:

"But you always said you were never interested in women."

I added:

"It's true, why do you change your mind all of a sudden?

John stared at his feet and replied:

"I don't know, I thought it would be a pity to die without having lived that experience. After all Matthias, you had a girlfriend yourself."

Matthias defended himself:

"Yes, but when we tried, it was a disaster. I couldn't even fuck her. I knew I was gay and that I was lying to myself. Poor girl..."

John kept staring at his feet and said:

"I just said it like that."

Then he changed the subject, but it was too late. The damage was done. My best friend whom I'd always fancied and who'd sworn he would never experiment, admitting he was tempted all of a sudden? I didn't need more for a crazy idea to flourish in my mind: why should we not have a child together, me and my gay best friend? Especially when we had sworn after a night when I had drunk far too much that if we had no kids ten years later, then we would have one together! And those ten years had gone by!

What an ideal combination! I have known him for twelve years. I am fairly certain he's STD free. He's gorgeous so the kid will be beautiful and when I get tired of hearing my child cry, I will give him to not one but two men who can care for him. The ticking of my biological clock would be gone… We could live all together in the same house and raise this child.

I knew Matthias didn't want to have children, whereas

John had always wanted kids but had given up the idea. But if I could make an old fantasy come true, then why not? I didn't realize that if I carried out this crazy idea, I would have to give up on the man of my dreams that I was so desperate to find. But the biological clock kept ticking and I knew I wanted to be pregnant at any cost.

I tossed and turned all night in bed, searching for ways to ask my best friend and his partner if they wanted to form a "family" with me. But I had to probe Matthias to find out if he had changed his mind. I needed to be careful.

The morning after—as the night had not brought advice and diverted me from this project—I took advantage of the time John was having a shower to put the tricky question:

"Tell me Matthias, you are still against the idea of having children, both of you?"

"Er... no. I think John gave up on the idea. He knows I don't want any and I think he's ok with it now."

"Ah, it's strange, I thought it was one of his great regrets."

"Not anymore. He understood that a child comes with a lot of responsibilities, that we couldn't go away on weekends whenever we want like we do so often, that we could not sleep anymore..."

Shit, this conversation didn't go at all in the direction I thought it would...

"What about you? Matthias asked. Last time I saw you, you kept talking about this new technique to freeze your eggs. Did you do it in the end?"

"No."

"You keep on waiting for the big love."

"Yes and at the same time I don't think he will come anymore. It's been two years now that the so-called man of my life left me, and honestly, I only throw myself at men who are panicked about commitment. Seriously this is the bad thing about this generation. Nobody wants to marry, let alone move in together or have children. I don't know where you find men who want to start a family, but they don't seem to be in Paris."

"I'm not worried about you You will find him."

"You are all so sweet to say this. OK but when? I was convinced that at 30, everything would be under control: a loving partner, two kids and a successful career. Seriously, it's depressing."

"You'll see, you will find him. As a matter of fact, John and I wanted to introduce you to someone. We're going to have lunch with him tomorrow. He's a friend of ours. I'm sure you're going to love him! And to top it all, he loves children."

"Who's that?!"

"Tsss. I have said too much already, it's a surprise…"

After that conversation with Matthias, I had called my best friend Luana. Once we had returned from Mexico, she had settled down quickly and had her first child soon after.

"Hey Luana, how are you?"

"I'm fine and you? I have terrific news for you."

From her tone, what she was going to say was obvious.

"You are pregnant with your second child?"

"How did you guess?"

"I don't know. Intuition. Congratulations!"

And there it was: the twinge. Like every time a friend told me she was pregnant. I was mad at myself to think this when I should have felt only bliss for them. But deep inside of me, I was envious and so jealous. They had succeeded where I had failed miserably. They had their loving partner and kids too. And I was still at the same point. I let go of my inner torment for a moment to ask:

"When are you due?"

"Well, I should have waited before telling you because it's only been a month. But I was so impatient to break the news that my boyfriend told me: "Ok, but you only say it to your best friend."

"I promise I won't say a word. And are you OK? Do you have any unpleasant symptoms?"

"I have terrible morning sickness. Nothing like my first pregnancy that went without a hitch. You'll see when it's your turn..."

How I hated this sentence... As if my best friend and all the others could predict that it would happen for me too. Given my situation, nothing was less sure.

"You know, I'm with a gay couple for the weekend so..."

"Oh, you're with Matthias and John? Sorry, I don't feel well."

She had hung up without saying goodbye... At least the only thing I could rejoice about while being single, was that I didn't feel sick and that I could enjoy a weekend by the sea with friends.

We spent the rest of the day walking along the coast without talking about babies. I realized I had once more built some castles in the air, a little bit too hastily as always.

Now that I really thought about it, it would be complicated with the custody of the child, we would have to live the three of us together and most of all Matthias would have to change his mind on the subject. It was not going to happen.

That evening, my crazy imagination was already invaded by an altogether different matter: my curiosity for that bachelor friend had reached its peak. I had tried to know more but John and Matthias were determined to say no more.

"At least you could tell me what he looks like!"

"You'll see!"

"But why haven't I ever met him before?"

"Because it's not been long since we started seeing him regularly."

"But why don't you say anything? I won't be able to wait until tomorrow. Do you have a picture? A clue, something?"

"No."

"But he lives in Normandy?"

"Julia, no more questions about our mystery man, it's time for an apéritif! And that's more important right now, isn't it?"

The sun was setting. We went to the café just off the beach, where we go every time I spend a weekend in their cottage at Le Tréport. The kind with sea decorations everywhere, lighthouse pictures, marine knots, model ships, the lot!

We were practically the only customers apart from two old men at the bar and the café owner: Martin. The Paris Saint Germain vs. Caen soccer game was on at 8.30pm and the regulars would come a little later. Martin welcomed us with a big smile.

"Hello you Parisians, we haven't seen you for quite a while!"

"Don't shout too loudly, there's a Paris Saint Germain vs. Caen game on tonight. We try to go unnoticed."

"Oh, but that's impossible my dears. We can recognize Parisians from afar. I don't know if it's the way you walk, the style or the accent, but no one will take you for a Norman here."

"What about John? He was born here…"

"It doesn't count. He's been too long in Paris now. In any case, you're going to lose."

On hostile ground, we didn't dare contradict him. John said:

"It's true that the Paris Saint Germain team isn't in great shape at the moment.

It was manna to the ears of an old man at the bar who said:

"The calva is on me!"

Without those first shots and all the others that followed that night, the course of our lives wouldn't have changed so dramatically.

The Normans, so happy to see we were losing, bought us drinks every time a goal was scored. Paris Saint Germain lost three nil and to thank us for having lost so miserably, they kept on offering us shots of calvados. I can't remember how many we downed. After ten, I had stopped counting. The Normans at the bar were laughing and so were we! It was 10.30pm when the match ended and half an hour later, we were past it. We had eaten nothing apart from a few peanuts.

One of the old men at the bar offered to drive us back in his car given our state, but he had drunk far more than we had. It was only three hundred meters' walk to the cottage anyway.

John and Matthias took my arms to help me walk. I was totally pissed. They were too, but they were carrying their alcohol better than I was.

I felt John's body against mine. I had never been so close to him or to Matthias for that matter. But all my body concentrated on its right side, where John was holding me. I was taking advantage of the situation to feel his warmth and all of his movements. The cottage was finally in sight and I started feeling really bad. I paled.

"I don't feel well. I think I'm going to throw up."

"Right now or can you wait till you get to the loo?"

"I can wait, but hurry up and open the door."

He rummaged in his pockets and took the key out. Luckily for me, there were two bathrooms in the cottage: one downstairs and one upstairs where the boys had their room. John opened and I rushed to the toilet while he switched on the light.

"Look after her, won't you John?" Matthias said, sounding disgusted as I was retched. "I'm so drunk, I'll go to bed right away if you don't mind."

Matthias kissed John while I was retching. I heard him going up to their room.

"I'll be as fast as I can, love." John replied.

"Given my state, I don't even think I will hear you when you get back in our room".

I felt John's hand gather my hair in a pony tail. I felt so ashamed that he should see me in that state, but I was so exhausted that I didn't have the courage to tell him to leave and standing was out of the question.

The scene probably lasted ten minutes, I don't know. All that time, John maintained my hair with one hand while soothingly stroking my back.

"I'm so sorry, I don't drink that much usually."

"Are you kidding? Can't you remember when we were out together?"

"Yes, but that was long ago. I don't get drunk that much nowadays."

"Don't worry, it's OK. I'm here."

"Please John, could you bring me a glass of water?"

"I bring you that right away. Don't move."

"It's not as if I could…"

He came back with a glass of water. I drank it very slowly. I hadn't sobered up at all. And in that case, it was better to hold my tongue… Last time I'd been in that state, we'd promised each other to have a child together ten years later.

"You must think I'm awful…"

"Don't worry. Oddly you're still pretty even when you're drunk, you know?"

"Stop making fun of me!"

"It's true, apart from that little rest of vomit at the corner of your mouth, you are so cute…"

I passed my hand on my mouth to remove the vomit but there was nothing there. Then with a lot of efforts I managed to stand up to remove the vomit but I couldn't see anything. John was making fun of me.

"And you find that funny?"

"Sorry my dear. Come here."

He took me in his arms and kissed my cheek to apologize.

"When you say you find me pretty, do you really think so?"

"Of course, I do."

"You never told me that before."

"I never had the occasion."

"And this idea to do it with a girl, what's the matter with you?"

"I don't know. Maybe it's a bit like you when you did it with a girl: to be sure, or simply not to die without knowing."

"And if you were to do it with a girl, would I be on your list?"

"Er, I hadn't thought about it... I don't think so. I'd rather do it with someone I don't know, I think. I wouldn't want it to ruin our friendship. Anyway it's just a stupid idea.

"Ah."

"Are you disappointed?"

"A little. And children? Would you have kids with me?"

When drunk, there was no way I could censor my words.

"What do you mean, children?"

"A couple of days ago, I read an article at my dentist's on these couples of gays and lesbians who share a house and children together."

"Are you a lesbian?"

"No! But you know, guys jerk off, they put the sperm in a syringe, and then the lesbians inject it while holding their legs up for an hour. They do that every time they ovulate until they get pregnant."

"Yes, I know this process."

"So what are we waiting for? Don't you want to do that? You said it yourself, you find me pretty. I've always thought you were handsome. We could live together and have a baby, couldn't we? And we had sworn that if we had no children after ten years, we would have them together, hadn't we?"

Me and my big mouth! John said:

"Yes, I remember we said that... And you were pretty much in the same state as tonight. Julia, I think you're not in your usual state. Won't you have a little more water?"

I drank what was left and then, I didn't have the time to reach the loo. I threw up the remnants of our evening on both of us.

"Julia, are you ok?!"

"I'm sorry. I didn't want to vomit on you."

"It's OK, I didn't like that T-shirt anyway," he said while he took it off.

"Now it's your turn."

"I don't think I'll be able to take my clothes off on my own."

"OK, let me help you."

He took away my dripping t-shirt. I was in my bra in front of him and still drunk as hell.

"Well, now that you're half naked, I think it would be better to take a shower. Don't go worry that anything will happen. I'm just going to help you take your shower because I know you can't stand up. And I will need one too otherwise Matthias will throw me out of bed with this horrendous smell."

He helped me undress slowly and carried me in the shower. Then he got rid of his own clothes while holding me up in his arms to keep me from falling. Even in my comatose state, I couldn't get my eyes off of him. His naked and chiseled body...

But when his eyes met mine, I pretended I didn't see anything. It was really a pity that he didn't like women! I was at the same time excited, still high from the alcohol and profoundly sad that life was so unfair.

He started to put soap on my neck and then my breast almost medically. He scrubbed my belly and my legs. He did the same for his torso while holding me in his arms. That's when I couldn't believe my eyes: he had a hard-on. He saw I had noticed and turned the water cold. I let a cry out out of surprise.

"It will sober you up," he justified.

I wasn't the only one to need it! After he showered us with cold water, he helped me out and took a clean towel from the cupboard while holding me on his right side. He wrapped it around me and rubbed my skin, then sat me down on the stool while he rubbed himself dry. Then he put his towel around his waist and asked me:

"Do you want to brush your teeth or shall I put you in your bed right away?"

"I'd like to brush my teeth."

"Can you stand over the basin?"

"Yes."

While I was brushing my teeth, I saw him one last time naked in the mirror because his towel had fallen down. No hard-on. Could I have dreamt it?

CHAPTER 3
EMMANUEL

The following morning, I woke up with the greatest hangover ever. My watch said 10.09am. I was naked under the sheets and I couldn't remember how I had ended up in my bed. I was emerging slowly, when little by little, some inglorious snippets of the night before came back to my mind, to the point I didn't dare get out of my room. What would John think of me? I had better shut up.

In the daylight, my great plan to have a baby with my best friend seemed completely absurd. I would have become a single mum in need of love and it wouldn't have been easy to explain to the kid that he had two fathers. Even less why...

Well, I dragged myself out of bed and put on my pyjamas. Matthias and John were sitting and eating breakfast. Matthias saw me first.

"Did you sleep well?"

With my husky morning voice, I answered:

"Like a baby. Do you have any aspirin?"

"I'll go and get you some," John said standing.

Matthias smiled and said:

"John told me you threw up."

Oh no, I thought, let's hope he didn't say anything more... I stammered:

"Let's say I wasn't at my best last night."

"Your clothes are in the washing-machine. I'll put them in the dryer right after so you can take them back to Paris."

I thanked him.

"I felt sorry for your neighbour on the train this afternoon… Are you hungry?"

"I'm starving."

I had started to eat when John came back with some aspirin. His mobile vibrated. He went to take it and talked to whoever was at the other end.

"It's Emmanuel. He's coming at 1pm. He's asking what to bring."

Matthias said sarcastically:

"A dessert? I think we'll avoid wine for lunch, won't you Julia?"

I glared at him before laughing.

"So that's his name? Emmanuel?"

"Don't look at me that way, I have no right to say anything."

John hung up. So I cried out:

"So, are you finally going to brief me or am I entitled to absolutely nada before he arrives? And besides, why all the secrecy?"

"Because every time we want to introduce you to a guy, you ask us everything about him, and when we show you a picture you say: "Nope, not my type." said John.

"Of course, why waste time meeting someone whom I don't like?"

John put his hand on Matthias' shoulder.

"Yes, but we are certain this time to have found a rare gem, aren't we Matthias?"

"Yes, this one, we're pretty sure you're gonna fall head over heels in love with him. He's totally your type."

"Hush! Don't say that, you're giving too much away. We said we would observe complete silence."

"He'll be there in less than two hours and she can't get away. So we might as well spill the beans…"

They exchanged a knowing look.

"Then what are you waiting for?"

For once they had hit the mark. Emmanuel was totally

my type: a tall brown-haired man with hazel eyes and shoulder-length curly hair.

HOT!

There he was, dressed in white trousers and a pea jacket. If I had been told he was a model for Jean-Paul Gaultier, I couldn't have been more struck by his beauty.

Apparently, on a previous visit to the cottage, Emmanuel had stopped in front of the photo on the fridge where John and I were smiling. He had asked who I was.

Emmanuel had removed his coat. Oh my! He was wearing a close-fitting white sweater and I could see his abs underneath. He sported a small three-day-old beard and when he smiled I think everything started to melt inside me. He stepped forward while I was still in shock.

I didn't expect at all such a physical blast when his cheek brushed against mine as he kissed me the French way to say hello. I think my face became red, while my body started yelling with all its might that it wanted more. When his eyes met mine, I started to shiver.

"Hi, I'm Emmanuel. I have heard so much about you, Julia."

I remained silent for what seemed an eternity. Given my head after our heavy drinking of the night before, I was wondering how he could find anything attractive in me. I had tried to improve things with make up, but I still didn't look my best. John gave me a nudge:

"Are you OK? Have you lost your tongue?"

I started to talk mechanically:

"What? Er... No. What do you mean? What did they tell you?"

"That you were fantastic."

Is it a joke? It's not possible, I said:

"What else?"

"That you were very pretty... And that I was your style of man."

What were these uncontrollable shivers that were

invading me?

"No, but seriously what is this conspiracy?"

"There isn't one... And they didn't lie."

His mouth came closer to my ear and whispered:

"You're much prettier in the flesh."

I think my red tomato colour started going scarlet. The sensation of his breathing against my ear left me with only one desire: to kiss him immediately. I saw Matthias pop his head round the kitchen door.

"Time to eat everybody, you will not let my soufflé go down, will you?"

Emmanuel took my hand.

"Let's go."

I was shivering beyond my control. In my stomach butterflies started flapping at the touch of his hand. I didn't dare look at him. I searched for John's eyes who smiled at me triumphantly as if to say: "You see, I think I've finally found you the one!"

Emmanuel sat down in front of me. I didn't remember being so instantly charmed by someone, nor saying so many useless sentences given how troubled I was. I wanted to shut up, but Emmanuel didn't make it easier with all his questions. I was trying to bring the conversation round to other topics but he always brought it back to me.

I could only gather that John and he had now been colleagues for three months, that Emmanuel had just finished his trial period, that he was a graphic designer and that John and Emmanuel had known each other since childhood. John had been in the same class as Paul, Emmanuel's brother. When Emmanuel came for dinner one night at John and Matthias' cottage and when Emmanuel saw my picture on the fridge, he fell head over heels for me and begged John to invite me so we could meet.

John had shown him all of the pictures he had of me in

his possession–I feared the worst–and he had told him that I was ready to do anything to find a man willing to start a family. How awful!

Emmanuel had been in a relationship that had recently broken down, and although he was two years younger than me, he had always wanted to have children.

His family often made fun of him because he still wasn't a father at 31. All his relatives were married and had already two or three children. So Emmanuel was desperately looking for the one... He found Parisian girls quite superficial and often they didn't want to commit themselves. Exactly what I thought of Parisian men!

It was too good to be true... When would John and Matthias admit that it was a joke, that this man was an actor who performed really well? Because for me, it was like a tsunami inside. Was it what people call love at first sight?

I didn't know how to react to so much attention from Emmanuel who seemed to devour me whole with only his eyes. It was as if he couldn't believe I was sitting in front of him. Neither could I.

I asked for some salt. Emmanuel passed me the salt cellar. His fingers touched mine and my cheeks went scarlet. I wanted John and Matthias to leave us alone so I could jump on him. I kept observing hos hands and then his neck where I wanted to cover him with kisses.

"Julia, would you like some water?"

Matthias had already asked me twice, but I had ignored him, lost in my contemplation of Emmanuel.

"Er...yes, please."

"Because it would do good things for your hangover."

"Are you ever gonna stop bringing up that subject?"

"We'll do so as long as we see that you're in this state... Some more calvados, Julia?"

I was sulking. I couldn't even remember what had happened the night before. As a result, I started to watch

John hoping it would help me remember the details...

All of a sudden I had a flash of John naked in the shower and I wondered why. I also vaguely remembered talking about my project to have a baby with him between two waves of vomit. Which had caused my shame when I woke up and realized I spoken this idea out loud. The image of him naked didn't match with the rest. Would that explain why I woke up naked under my sheets, when I normally always wear pyjamas? I started panicking.

All of that seemed more than real. Looking at John, I tried to understand how I could have such a precise vision of his body, when I had never seen him shirtless except on a beach in a swimsuit. John looked away and got up to get some cheese from the kitchen. I followed him there leaving Matthias and Emmanuel alone. Once out of reach, I asked:

"John, what really happened last night?"

He turned towards me surprised.

"What do you mean?"

"I don't remember anything between the bathroom and when I woke up naked in my bed this morning."

"Really?! Nothing at all?"

"Nope! outside the fact that I had a vision of you..."

I shook my head.

"No, it can't be possible..."

"What?"

"Could it be that we were naked in the shower you and I last night? It makes no sense…"

"Listen, I think we need to talk just the two of us. Why don't we meet for coffee together next week, OK?"

"Er... Ok. But why can't we talk about it now?"

"Don't panic, nothing serious happened."

"Are you sure?"

"Totally sure."

He seemed uncomfortable and looked at the ground, then he pointed at the dresser.

"Take some plates and knives. I'll take care of the cheese tray and the bread."

He didn't reassure me at all. Was it possible that we had ended up making love together? How could he do that to me the night before and then introduce me to the perfect man? I was so mad at myself for not remembering anything because if I had made love to my gay best friend−a lifetime fantasy−I would have wanted to savour it to the last drop...

I came back at the table. My face must have looked worried because Emmanuel asked me right away:

"You don't seem well."

"I think it's the backlash from yesterday."

"We're going to have a walk on the beach after lunch. It will help to breathe some sea air."

I turned towards Matthias and John.

"Are you sure we need some more cheese after a... cheese soufflé?"

"You're in Normandy my dear, Camembert is *de rigueur*. Unless you prefer... a *trou normand*?"

And the three of them burst with laughter... I couldn't see myself having that mix of apple sherbet and calvados that you are offered in between courses to help make way for the next ones.

"Ah, ah, ah... No, it'll be all right. I could throw up just smelling it. I will pass on the Camembert. I'll eat dessert though."

I turned towards Emmanuel... Would I finally stop shivering every time I laid my eyes on him or what?

Lunch went on in between jokes on my drunkenness from the night before and questions about my work, my parents, my childhood... Emmanuel wanted to know everything. But I couldn't help remembering what I had seen in the shower. John had been sexually aroused. I was sure of it now. And that troubled me a lot to say the least. How could he have had an erection when he wasn't attracted to girls?

After this copious meal, I only wanted one thing: a nap. I was still hungover and the aspirin didn't do much to improve my state.

Furthermore, digestion only aggravated the symptoms of advanced drowsiness I felt. Only the presence of Emmanuel maintained me afloat. I was under the impression he was a mirage, a figment of my imagination just like the vision of John naked in the shower.

The weather was fantastic on that day. Some high clouds troubled the blue sky and we were all wearing sunglasses because the intensity of the light on the sand was blinding us. It was too cold to go and bathe as this was early April. Although they were a couple, Matthias and John didn't walk arm in arm. They were conscious that not everyone was open to gay couples in the region and they preferred to keep any sign of intimacy private. I found it sad not to be able to express oneself physically like any other heterosexual couple.

Emmanuel had offered me his arm and I concentrated on his touch. I was feeling hysterical but tried not to show it by talking about the weather:

"It's really cold in this country... I wonder why the Normans invaded this part instead of going further down south."

Matthias answered:

"Well...they tasted calvados and never managed to leave. A bit like you my dear."

"But I'm leaving later on..."

Emmanuel looked at me intensely, visibly disappointed and exclaimed:

"What a pity!"

"Why? Are you staying?" I asked him.

"Yes, I took Monday off, it's my father's birthday tonight and I only go back tomorrow. That's why I only came to meet you now; otherwise I would have come earlier. But John told me it was your only free week-end for a long time, so we arranged things this way."

I turned towards John and Matthias:

"How long have you been organizing all this, you little schemers?"

John looked at Matthias with a grin before answering:

"Well... For three weeks I think."

"How come you didn't tell me anything, John?"

"Well that wouldn't have been a surprise otherwise... And we know you: you would have invented an excuse to leave on an earlier train. Now you're stuck with us..."

Emmanuel stopped to ask:

"What time does your train leave exactly?"

"At 4.38pm."

Emmanuel plunged his eyes into mine and said:

"It's such a pity you can't stay longer."

My body started melting.

*
* *

The three of them had seen me off to the train station. It was time to kiss Emmanuel goodbye and I couldn't believe my reaction. My heart was beating so fast for this man I didn't know a few hours before. His lips trailed on my cheek.

"Can I see you in Paris?" he asked.

"Yes. John will give you my number..."

Emmanuel looked at his feet and admitted:

"I already asked him."

John patted my shoulder.

"Be careful, he's the kind who harasses girls."

This time, Emmanuel was the one who patted John's shoulder.

"What are you talking about?"

Then Emmanuel turned towards me:

"If you're free tomorrow night, I'd like to take you out for dinner."

"I'll think about it."

"Come on, say yes!"

"I really need to get on the train, otherwise it will leave without me."

Emmanuel gave me the saddest smile and waved goodbye.

Once aboard, I almost wanted to get off and run into his arms. After all, I could have driven back to Paris with Matthias and John a bit later. Especially when nothing interesting awaited me home on a Sunday evening in Paris, apart from cleaning my flat, which I would certainly end up not doing. Well, if Emmanuel was about to show up tomorrow evening, I would have to do it. It had been three weeks since I had last tidied up and it was really a mess. Before the door closed I yelled to Emmanuel:

"All right, it's a yes!"

It was as if my mouth had pronounced these words on their own accord. And as if my body was on automatic pilot as soon as I had seen him. I nevertheless felt the need to be alone to clarify everything that had happened over the last hours. In the train, I fell asleep like a baby to the point where my neighbour had to wake me up when we arrived at the Gare Montparnasse terminus. I was dreaming that John and I were making love. Decidedly, something was quite wrong if my unconscious kept bringing it back to the surface of my mind!

I looked at my cell while walking and avoided a signpost on the platform at the very last second when I read the message:

> Julia, you are beyond any description John may have made of you. I'm dying to see you tomorrow. I'll pick you up at 8pm. PS: by the way

yes, I also asked John for your address...

"The stalker kind", John said? If all the good-looking men I had come across that last couple of years could have had harassed me that way instead of me chasing them...

I carried on walking on the platform with a broad smile. I didn't want to reply right away. I preferred to wait and be home to think calmly about how I would answer. I had found Emmanuel magnificent, but his way to treating me as if I was already his, as if he didn't doubt one second that we were meant for one another had charmed, seduced and annoyed me at the same time. He acted as if he'd never doubted I would be attracted to him. Maybe my perpetual blushing in his presence had betrayed me? At the same time I thought it was just too good to be true. There was something fishy. I carried on thinking that the boys had paid an actor to trick me. It was impossible otherwise. It was obvious that a man like that couldn't be interested in me. And I didn't say that just because he was damn handsome.

He also was very eloquent and when he had shown me his portfolio of drawings on his cell, I understood right away that I was face to face with a real artist. Probably as gifted as my father who was a painter, but in a totally different genre. I had simply never met a guy who acted this way. It had to be a comedian or he had some hidden fault somewhere…

I had to find out. I called John. Damn his voice mail! Either he was busy with something else or he was avoiding me. A little like in the kitchen earlier on.

I couldn't help thinking that we must have ended up making love that Saturday night even if I couldn't remember it. But if it was the case, I should have at least felt it. Yes my body should have remembered that. But I couldn't feel anything. Was it my hangover that concentrated all of my sensations solely on the headache that assailed me? And why did I have this image of him naked in the shower, completely disconnected of the rest of my memories? I was sure I hadn't dreamt it. I left a message on the answering machine.

> Hello John, it's me. Come on, spit it out, Emmanuel is an actor, isn't he? The more I think about it, the more I believe you have paid him to have a good laugh about me! He's really good in any case, I must say bravo. I really need to see you tomorrow. Tell me if we can have lunch. I'll come and get you at work...

I was disappointed that he didn't answer. Disappointed, remaining with my doubts. I got back home around 7pm. Alone, my fridge almost empty and my stomach asking desperately for food even after this giant Norman luncheon. I decided to go to the supermarket. On my way, I thought about what I missed the most when being single: it was not to have someone to kiss when I came home. Someone to tell about my week-end. Someone who had cooked something really good while waiting for me and who told me he had missed me.

I was too lazy to clean up my flat. I looked at Emmanuel's text once more. I decided not to answer before I could see John to make sure it wasn't a joke. Although Emmanuel seemed so sincere. And what I had felt when he brushed my skin had driven me crazy. Like something animal, instinctive. I wanted him. Oh and to hell with it! I changed my mind and answered his message:

> I don't mind. See you tomorrow night!

CHAPTER 4
A MONDAY LIKE NO OTHER

My alarm clock had rung, but the headache persisted and I had gone back to sleep. When I opened my eyes, it took me a good five minutes to realize it was Monday. As a result, I was late. The day was starting badly.

When you must travel on the Paris metro's line 13, you never know when you're going to be able to squeeze in. Especially when I had a really important meeting with a client for the launch of a website project. I jostled and managed to get aboard the first train. A real feat at that time of the day! But while waiting, squeezed like a sardine in its tin, it was impossible to look at my telephone and to know if John had answered me. I took it easy by observing people. There were decidedly no decent men there, only celery! I was seeing Emmanuel tonight, so it didn't matter so much anymore...

Why was it so hard to find someone? Would I end up like a cousin who only found her husband after she turned fifty and had had no children? Though I had found tasty heterosexuals in the chocolate cake style. But they had always left. I think it was too obvious that I wanted everything right away. Children especially. And that made them all run away...

Why is it taboo for men when for us women, when we kiss a guy, the first thing we think about is if we're going to marry him and have children? Well for me that was always the case anyway, but maybe I was an exception?

Station *La Fourche*. I somehow managed to get off the metro, but on the platform, hordes of people were queuing to get out. I managed to glance at my phone. Still no message. I elbowed my way through the crowd like only Parisians know how, in haste and without excuses nor thank yous.

I arrived breathless and sweaty in my office building: I had managed to be only ten minutes late. In the staircase, I glanced a last time at my smartphone. No news from John; I typed a text quickly.

> I'll meet you at 1pm at your office. We'll go to the trattoria round the corner and then to the park, the weather is so beautiful!

I had reached my floor. Sandra, the switchboard operator, waved her hand while answering the phone, her headset screwed onto her head. She gave me big eyes, which meant in our coded language that my boss, Rémi, was already there. Damn it, I didn't want him to see that I was late again... As I was thinking that, he came out of the open space to go and have a coffee with my colleague, Lauren, who still hadn't stomached the fact I had been promoted project manager and not her.

"Good morning Julia, so what's your excuse today?" he asked.

"I went back to sleep, I thought it was Sunday."

"It's high time you learnt how to count the days of the week at your age..."

My boss was making fun of me, but Lauren's sneer was one of a hyena ready to bite.

"At least you didn't forget we have a meeting with Daltigneau at 10am? Everything's ready?"

"Almost. I need to reprint the presentation, and to read the contract one last time before printing it..."

I got to my desk and pushed the start button of my computer. Nothing happened. I pushed it again. Nothing. Such a lucky morning! My computer had to crash at that peculiar moment. As if by accident. It was already 9.17am and I picked up the phone to call my faithful computer maintenance troubleshooter Momo:

"Hey there beautiful, what's the matter?" he asked.

"My computer is crashing again. Same symptoms as last time. I thought you had put a competition processor and that this shouldn't happen anymore?"

"Er you know machines live their own life. I revive them but they sometimes make suicide attempts again. Give me five minutes."

What could I do in between? I went straight to the coffee machine. I didn't have time to drink or eat anything. I passed by my colleague Lauren, who was coming back with hers in hand. I announced her the sad news:

"My computer won't start."

She smiled and then started whining.

"Oh, you really have no luck, she said pretending to sympathize with me what are you going to do for your presentation?"

I hated her. There were slaps I was dying to give her.

"As a matter of fact, I copied you onto the email for Rémi, could you send me the latest version of the presentation and the contract on my personal email please?"

I hoped she would actually do it: Lauren always chose to be at her meanest. There was a time though, when we had been great friends. Until the day she noticed that Arthur the accountant was hitting on me: she had a crush on him. In the following month, I had gone from Assistant to Project Manager: she wanted the job too. I had got it because I deserved it, but she was certain she should have had it.

Hence her strategic alignment with Rémi, my boss. She systematically pointed out my being late, something I never did for her. But my work had always been done and very well done. Often, I even stayed late to catch up.

Rémi knew it and made fun of me but in truth we had always got along. I came back with a hot coffee in my hands. I was going towards the open space when Alex, my trainee, opened the door to it in one go and in the process spilled the coffee over my white blouse, burning me in the process.

Great: late, headache, computer crashed, blouse stained and no change of clothes. I only needed John to call me and say that he couldn't meet me, that Emmanuel admitted tonight than the boys had paid him to play a practical joke on me and the day would be perfect!

Everyone in the open space was laughing and I realized that my blouse which was only slightly transparent before revealed everything now. My only solution was to go to the wash-room to try and repair this gaffe. I rinsed the blouse's stain in the sink and rubbed it with soap. I pretty much managed to make it go away but the blouse was partly damp with water. I wrung it out, but the three minutes of ironing from the day before were definitely ruined: the blouse was crumpled. Luckily for me we had kept the good old hand dryers like the ones in Madonna's *Desperately Seeking Susan...* But it would take hours so I hung it and started to rub my bra with soap.

I looked at my watch: 9.32am. I hoped that Momo had succeeded in reviving my computer and that perhaps Lauren for once would have taken pity on me... or that Alex, the intern, for the first time in four months, had showed some initiative at last by printing the presentation and the contracts. I could dream... I had tried to empower him all along so that he could make his own decisions but he had always worked in the mode "I need to ask permission from my boss before doing anything..."

Too bad, it was time to go back. You could see everything through my blouse so I hurried back to my desk and put on my jacket: it would be hot, but the stain would be less visible.

When I arrived, I saw Momo in front of my computer.

"Still not working?"

"No, but I think I know what's wrong. I will need to reinstall some softwares. It will take another hour."

"Shit! Sorry, it's just that I really needed it now. Right away. Without delay."

"You know how these things are, always calling sick when you need them."

I turned towards Lauren.

"Lauren, were you able to send me the documents?"

"Oh, sorry! The phone kept on ringing. I totally forgot. I'll do it now."

What a sneaky creep!

I came out of the open space and went directly to the coffee machine where my boss and my client were waiting for me. The meeting went well, which was a relief for me. The client was convinced and had signed the contract. I could now relax. Maybe this run of bad luck which had ben going the whole morning on me had finally stopped?

I was dying to know if John had replied. And I had received a text…

> Not available for lunch, my dear. We can grab a coffee after work, but I can't stay more than an hour.

That meant we would meet at the *Café des Phares* in Bastille. The rest of the day went by without any more incidents.

I didn't know how to broach the subject with John. After all, he had drunk as much as me on that fateful evening, maybe he had forgotten everything too? After arriving at the café, I found a place on the terrace. John hadn't arrived yet. I looked at my new messages, but I had only obvious spam in my emails in the style of «enlarge your penis» and "make your wife come all night with Viagra"... Highly targeted emails!

It was a warm spring day. I shrugged off my jacket down and now everybody could see my stained blouse, but I couldn't care less. At last John arrived.

"Hey... What happened?" he said looking at my blouse.

"Long story... Let's say I went from catastrophe to catastrophe today... In the end, the intern spilled red hot coffee on me. So, it was a really nice day as you can see.

"Indeed, I'm surprised you have survived until now to tell the tale…"

The waiter arrived.

"What will it be?"

"Peppermint cordial with water, please" I said.

"And a coffee. Thanks."

The waiter gone, John turned towards me saying:

"Well, that's a change from a little red wine for an aperitif. Peppermint cordial? Want to be reminded of your childhood?"

"No, but after yesterday's hangover, I may just as well stop drinking alcohol for the rest of my life."

"Until next time…"

I burst out laughing.

"Maybe. We don't have much time so I need to know everything about Emmanuel. First, is he an actor or not?"

"Do you really think I would play such a joke on you, when you've been looking for the man of your dreams for years?"

"Let's say his behaviour seemed so... No one has ever acted as if I was the woman of his life at first sight. What did you do to him, did you put a spell on him?"

"No, I just talked to him about you and showed pictures of you. He's the one who reacted instantly."

"Is that all?"

"Yes. He just got hooked and I told him that you weren't looking for a one-night-stand, but rather for the man of your dreams, the one with whom you would have children."

"And he didn't run away?"

"No, on the contrary, it's exactly what he's looking for. He's made for you. He only falls for girls who find him very cute, who stay a little with him, but who in the end find him too nice. And you know girls better than me, there is a little masochistic tendency to love bad boys. You, for example, you only go out with that type…"

"Well that's because I never find a nice looking man who's also nice. In general, good-looking equals bad boy and nice equals average-looking. If Emmanuel is the guy you say he is, it's the first specimen I've ever met in my entire life. I mean apart from you, but you are..."

"... Gay?"

"I would rather say inaccessible."

There was a silence between us. It's as if I was confessing I had a crush on him, though I knew nothing would ever happen.

"Are you sure he's exactly like the description you just gave of him? I mean, he must have a flaw, something…"

"If you only knew how certain I am. I've known Emmanuel since he was a child. We have many friends in common and I know his parents too. They all say the same: the ideal husband. And I don't only say that because he cooks like a god."

"But that's too good to be true!"

"No my dear, good things come to those who wait. As a matter of fact, he kept on talking about you after you left, saying how prettier you were in reality than on the photos and that he was dying to see you again. I think indirectly you must have broken the hearts of half the single female staff in my office."

"And you the other half?"

"Maybe…"

"But at the office, he never found someone?"

"No. He's got a rule: no love at work."

"But to mix childhood friends and work is ok?"

"I used to know his brother much better than him. So when I saw him arrive at the office, we had a common past and we got closer very quickly."

"Aren't you attracted to him?"

"I would lie if I didn't tell you that I find him cute. But I prefer his brother..."

I had to broach the subject, but I didn't know how.

"You know, about Saturday night..."

He looked at his feet for a bit before answering me.

"Yes?"

"I don't really remember what happened. I barely remember how we got home. I just remember vaguely you helped me throw up in the toilet bowl. Yesterday morning, I also remembered that I had talked to you about my wacky idea to have a child together and I wanted to apologize. I feel so ashamed."

"Julia, don't worry. I know how important it is to you to have children. It was for me too... And we made the promise to have one together ten years ago..."

"If we hadn't succeeded before. You haven't given up the idea, then?"

"I haven't, but Matthias is not too keen. And for us gay couples, it's a bit complicated. We must find a lesbian pair and share the custody or find a surrogate mother. Imagine we'd had a baby together and then you'd found the man of your dreams? It would have been a disaster, wouldn't it?"

"I don't know. I have a hard time knowing what would have happened. That can't happen anyway, I would know it if we'd had sex together, wouldn't I?"

I observed him while I was uttering this sentence. I would finally know if that image of him having a hard-on in the shower was real at last. John had a nervous little laugh.

Could it be that he didn't remember it either? He was my best friend. He had never lied. Why would he start today?

"In any case, you found the father of your children. I bet you and Emmanuel are married within the year."

"That's a bit quick. We've only known each other since yesterday and we barely know anything about one another. I still think he has some defect somewhere."

"Frankly, I know he stays for years with his girlfriends. He's the nice, faithful and attentive type. Your type."

"But why did they leave him then?"

"Well, that you will have to find out."

I looked at my watch. It was almost 7pm. I had to leave if I wanted to prepare myself to meet the so-called future man of my life…

"John, I gotta go. You too I believe?"

"Yes, I've got my yoga class tonight."

I left money on the table and kissed John goodbye before running to catch the bus, which was arriving at the nearby bus stop. Ten minutes later, I was home and sweaty.

I went straight to the shower. After the stress of the day, the heat from the water did me good and made me realize that the effects of Saturday night's hangover were gone at last. I dried my hair very quickly to have more time to concentrate on my make up and on the choice of the right outfit for the evening. I wanted to impress him. I opted for a little black dress and heels. I preferred not to take risks, in case he took me to a chic place. I was putting on a last touch of mascara right when the bell of the videophone started ringing.

"I'll be down in two minutes!", I said.

Considering the vaguely tidy condition of my flat, I preferred not to have him come up. Time to inspect myself a last time in the mirror and to put on my heels, I was ready at last. I hoped he would like the result.

Compared to yesterday's looks, it could only be better. I opened the door of the building. He was there wearing a suit, as beautiful as a god and he gave me a big smile when he saw me.

"You are breathtaking…"

I was the one to gasp. And the whole procession of shivers, red cheeks and butterflies in the stomach had resurfaced as I laid my eyes on him.

"So are you."

He lent to kiss me on both cheeks and stayed a little longer than expected on each. The contact of his skin made me shiver. It was beyond my control.

"Where are we going?"

"A surprise isn't a surprise if you unveil it."

"A little clue, then?"

"We are going on an island…"

"You're not taking me on an island in Normandy, are you?"

"No, not so far…"

He opened the door of his car and closed it when I was settled in. And besides he was a gentleman! He started the engine.

He drove along the banks of the Seine and I expected him to take me to the *île Saint Louis* or *île de la Cité*. But he kept driving. I was wondering about which island it could be… When we arrived at Neuilly, I understood we were going towards *île de la Jatte*. He parked on a street and rushed to open the door for me to help me get out. I thought I could really get used to all these attentions. While walking side by side, I didn't dare talking… I was content with breathing his smell and trying to guess each of his movements to, I must admit, try and brush his skin with impunity. I saw the front of a restaurant named *Les pieds dans l'eau*.

Emmanuel told the head waiter that he had booked a table for two. The place was rather posh and I was happy I had opted for something formal. He motioned us to follow him and brought us to the terrace which was literally *les pieds dans l'eau* that is to say feet in the water: on the border of the Seine right above the surface. It was breathtaking.

"This is an incredible place…"

"You like it too? And furthermore, the food is really good."

The waiter brought the menus. I opened mine and took advantage of Emmanuel being totally absorbed in reading it to observe him. It was crazy, but I had the feeling I had known him forever and most of all to be totally mad about him already. And the best was, it seemed reciprocal.

"Is there a dish you recommend?"

"Last time, I ate sea bass with a little homemade mashed potatoes and it was delicious."

"Are you having the same again?"

"No, tonight I'm gonna go for the turbot. But you should go for the sea bass."

"Let's go for the sea bass then."

The waiter arrived.

"Would you like to drink an apéritif?"

"No, thanks." I answered.

"No, but we're going to drink some wine."

He turned towards me.

"Well that is, if you want wine, Julia…"

"Yes, why not?"

And that's how my resolution not to drink had held only about forty eight hours…

"I understood that you were quite scalded by alcohol."

Would they ever leave me in peace with that hangover story?

"My resolution will have held two days only… Luckily I hadn't bet anything with John."

"I did! He owes me five euros!"

I looked at him, incredulous.

"I'm kidding... I just wanted to see your reaction..."

Great! He kept on laughing at my expense. Just like John and Matthias... It must be a national sport when you're a Norman... I turned my head towards the lights on the Seine.

"Did I upset you?"

"No."

"You're very quiet."

"I admire the view."

"Julia, I only dream of one thing, but I don't dare ask… I would like to take your hand in mine."

I certainly didn't expect that. After hesitating for aa fraction of a second I gave it to him.

"Will you give it back though?"

"Not sure. Maybe I've got a magical power that makes it impossible for you to detach yourself from me now."

"I'm not sure I dislike it entirely. It's just going to be uneasy to dress up and undress. And then… my colleagues are going to wonder why I'm going to work with you."

"Yes, but it's practical when you need me. I'll always be there right above your palm."

And he put his hand above mine. His contact made me shiver.

"Are you cold?"

"No."

"Do you want my jacket?"

"No, don't worry."

He stared at me and even though I wanted to lose myself in his eyes, I looked away. The waiter came. As a result I moved my hand away from Emmanuel's so that he could place the bottle on the table.

"Maybe one day I'll ask for it again", said Emmanuel.

The waiter poured some wine into Emmanuel's glass.

"What?", I asked.

He wet his lips and took a sip.

"Very good, thank you…"

The waiter finished filling the glasses and then went away. Emmanuel stared at me again.

"Your hand," he said.

Was I hallucinating or did he just say he would one day propose to me? No, he only meant he would take my hand in his later surely…

The rest of the evening was magical. Emmanuel told me everything about his life, from his flawless childhood in the city of Le Tréport, to his coming to Paris to study. I thought it was a little bit too early to ask the question, but I did anyway:

"But how come a man like you is single?"

He stared at me intensely and said:

"I was waiting for you…"

What a charmer… I felt like I was in a movie where all the lines were everything I had always dreamt of hearing.

"No but seriously Emmanuel…"

"I am dead serious, Julia. When I saw your picture in John's kitchen, I swear to you I had a crush. You will think it's crazy, but from that moment I knew you were… the woman of my life."

"Come on, this is what you say to all the girls you want to get into your bed."

"Julia, do I give you that impression? And most of all, didn't you feel the same way when we met yesterday?"

"What did you feel?"

"That I had always known you. And when our cheeks brushed, I felt something obvious."

I was in panic mode. That was impossible. He had described exactly how I had felt the night before with what could have been my own words.

"Do you know that I asked John if you were an actor?"
"Why?"

"Because I was convinced that John and Matthias paid you to trick me."

"Why would they do such a thing?"

"You know, they're teasing and I've been telling them for so many years that I'm looking for the man of my life to start a family with that I thought they'd paid you to play a joke on me."

"But why?"

"Because I can't believe that you are saying everything I've always wanted to hear and that I feel everything that you say…"

He got up, took my hand to make me get up and then he pulled me to him and kissed me. It was as if everything had vanished around us. I can't remember how long our kiss lasted. There was only him and me or more exactly his lips on mine, one hand caressing my hair while the other hugged me. I had never felt that good in someone's arms. To kiss him was a second moment of revelation after having touched him. The words of Emmanuel resounded in my ears: "I felt something obvious...".

He loosened his grip much to my dissatisfaction and whispered in my ear.

"Shall we go?"

"Yes."

"I'll bring you back home."

"Ok."

"It's on me."

I remained speechless. I knew I couldn't end the night without him. His kiss had awoken too many things in me. I needed to know everything about him. He helped me put my jacket back on and went to pay at the counter. Before going into the car, he gave me an even more languid kiss. Boy, how was it possible to fall in love with someone so quickly? I was looking at him while he was driving and was passing my hand through his hair. At each red light, he kissed me and we could hear horns to make us move forward because the light had turned green without us realizing it... While he was driving, I kept looking at him without being able to believe even an instant that this Adonis was crazy about me. At least, that's what he said... Maybe he just wanted to sleep with me and leave me like an old sock the following morning after telling me everything I wanted. But a little voice was telling me he was sincere. That what I was living was love at first sight. Two soul mates had met. I was sure about it. Emmanuel was the man I had been waiting for...

Always so gallant, he hastened to open the door of the car for me. Once I stood, he carried me and brought me to my door while kissing me. No man had ever done such thing to me. I could have remained hours nestled in his arms. He put me down once outside the building's entrance so that I could dial the code. In the lift, our kisses were becoming more urgent. I opened the door of my flat and after I closed it on us, I knew that night would change my life forever. Emmanuel kissed me passionately while I put my hand under his shirt. I felt his muscular back and moved both hands up its length to squeeze him tight against me as I kissed him. He stopped me abruptly.

"Julia, I won't do anything you don't want me to."

No, but seriously, how did he do that? Who was the mother of this perfect man? Or should I say Prince Charming?

"I believe there is nothing you could do I wouldn't want."

He smiled.

"Oh really? I brought my whip, shall I take it out?"

"Ok, maybe not that..."

He burst out laughing. I removed his jacket, and started to unbutton his shirt. The day before, I had been able to admire his sculpted torso under his t-shirt; when I removed his shirt, I thanked the Normans for having brought a man with such a beautiful body. I started to caress his muscled and slightly tanned torso. His skin was so soft...

"It's not fair, I'm half naked and you're still all dressed up…", he said.

I took a step back and started to run towards the bed.

"If you catch me, you have the right to remove everything."

Emmanuel chased me and made us fall on the bed laughing. He kissed me softly and then stood up to remove my jacket. He put his lips on my right hand then moved up my arm before doing the same with my left side.

He removed my shoes and caressed my feet, my calves and my thighs before pulling up my dress and removing it. He laid down while pulling me into his arms. I was shivering from head to toe as I felt his skin against mine.

"You're trembling."

"Yes, I believe you do a strange effect to me. Hey, I'm the one who's more naked than you now. It's not fair."

The rest of our clothes were removed in no time. His eyes, loaded with desire, examined me from head to toe and then he finished with a fiery kiss on my mouth.

"You're magnificent, Julia."

We were high from our caresses. I felt his desire going up every instant. I wanted to make one with him, right now.

"Do you have some?" he asked.

"Yes, I'll be right back."

I kissed him one last time, I was having such a hard time pulling myself away from his skin, then I headed for the bathroom. I found a condom and walked back to the bedroom.

What I felt for Emmanuel was not comparable to what I had experienced with other men up until that day. We were totally in fusion as if we were meant for each other. Our movements were in total harmony. Our first time was magical...

Except for one detail: when he withdrew, the condom

was not where it should have been. There was total panic and then it must be said too, shame... It had remained stuck. I rushed into the bathroom in what was certainly one of the least glamorous moments of my life. Not only did I almost cramp my hand by looking for the condom that was slipping from my fingers higher and higher, but in addition I realized with horror that I was in the middle of my cycle and I had not taken the pill for months...

Yes, I was dreaming of being a mother, but not like this, not so soon and not without being sure that my partner hadn't a sexually transmitted disease... The return to reality was shattering. I knew somehow that the bad luck from the morning hadn't gone that easily.

Emmanuel tapped at the door to know if everything was ok. I had finally succeeded in extracting the condom at the cost of improbable contortions. If our newborn couple could survive this, then we could survive anything. I left the bathroom. Emmanuel was waiting for me looking anxious. He had put his underwear and shirt back on. He took me in his arms.

"I have good and bad news", I muttered.

"Start with the good news."

"The good news is I recuperated the condom. The bad is I'm not on the pill and I'm most certainly in the middle of my cycle and that we haven't done an AIDS test. Personally I haven't done a test for a long time. As for you, I know nothing about your sexual past... It also means I must go get the morning after pill as soon as possible."

He put a finger on my mouth.

"Julia, look at me. I don't have AIDS, but I'm not asking you to take my word for it. We'll go get a test tomorrow morning first things to reassure us both, OK? As for the morning after pill, forget about it."

"What do you mean forget about it?"

"Julia, if tonight you get pregnant, then it would be the

best thing that could ever happen to us. I've been waiting for you for years. I know it's you. I've never felt anything like this for anyone else."

I was stunned. But where was this man coming from? From heaven, an envoy from heaven!

"Are you kidding me?"

"No, why?"

"Are you a Martian who came to make a poor little Earthling pregnant and recall the fruits of the experiment nine months later?"

"No."

"Did they put something special in your wine?"

"You drank the same so no."

"Ah yes, I know it, you were programmed to tell me all I ever dreamt of hearing."

He laughed then stared at me.

"Julia, I've never been so serious. Since I saw you yesterday, I'm like crazy. I'm mad with desire for you. I could spend the rest of my life in your arms."

"But you barely know me."

"Julia, my instinct tells me it's you. I finally found you. The woman of my life."

"You know that any other girl would run away on hearing such a thing."

"But not you."

"No, not me."

"Because you feel exactly the same."

"Exactly."

He pulled me to him and hugged me tight.

"If I tell you I love you already, are you going to run?" he asked.

No but really it was impossible that he could tell me that so soon... And yet that's exactly what I felt for him. I was already madly in love with him. I tried to get away from him to pretend I was going to run but he kept hugging me tightly. I tried again but he was still holding me tight.

"Why did you get dressed?" I asked.

"I don't know, by reflex."

"Well, since we're screwed, we might as well get back to it!"

I didn't have to tell him twice. That night was unforgettable. Not only because for the first time of my life, a man made love to me without being afraid of becoming a father, but also because I had the conviction I had finally found the man of my dreams… The run against the ticking clock was over and for once I hoped it would leave us time to get to know each other a bit more before starting a baby.

CHAPTER 5
AT LAST!

The following week went by like a total ecstasy. I think I had never slept so little without feeling tired. I arrived at work with unwavering smile despite the ever-renewed baseness of my colleague Lauren, who couldn't believe that I was so happy.

The day after our first night, we had taken the HIV test which to our great relief turned out negative. By the end of the week, Emmanuel had decreed he couldn't live without me. As his flat was bigger, I was the one who moved. I had always complained that I only ran into men who didn't want to commit, so I was always more amazed every day.

We had agreed that it was useless for me to take the pill again. I thought it would be impossible for me to be pregnant the first few times anyway. For all my friends, it had taken between six months and three years, so I didn't even bother to take a pregnancy test… I thought if I was, I would feel it. After all, my girlfriends all told me about breasts that hardened in the first few days, nausea, etc. I had none of that.

So it was a shock to see that I still hadn't got my period a week after the due date. I waited three more days, but still nothing. So I decided to take a pregnancy test bought in a pharmacy without telling Emmanuel one evening when he had not yet returned from work. I was in shock! It was positive...

I panicked and called my doctor to see him immediately. After all, the test was not 100% reliable. He asked me the date of the last day of my period and if I had a number of symptoms. He prescribed a blood test for me.

I came home late that night and Emmanuel, this love, had cooked lasagna in my absence. I texted him to tell him I had to go to the doctor urgently. I wasn't sure if I should break the news to him even though I wasn't 100% sure yet, but opening the door and seeing his gaze and huge smile, I could feel he somehow already knew.

In my haste, I had left the test box on the sink... He hugged me and spun me around while kissing me. Mad with joy was a weak word in the face of the joy of Emmanuel who covered me– what can I say, almost suffocated me!– with kisses without my being able to utter a word. I laughed because he kissed me whenever I wanted to say something. In the end, he put me back on the ground and took my hand to sit me down.

"I believe I'm pregnant", I said.

"That's what I thought I understood. But aren't you sure yet?

"No. I have to do a blood test tomorrow morning to confirm it.

I had gone for the blood test the next morning and the next twenty-four hours seemed to last forever. I decided to pick up the results before going to work so that I could take them to the doctor in the evening.

The results were positive. Who says you can't get pregnant having sex for the first time with your boyfriend? I was living proof. I was both overjoyed and a little panicked. It had all happened so quickly. Within a month, we had met, then settled down together and now I was pregnant!

Everything I had always looked for in a man, this commitment that I had so lacked as well as this romanticism, I had found in Emmanuel.

But I was afraid of the backlash. Afraid of discovering a nasty secret or a flaw that would make him unbearable to me... Everything was too good to be true... In front of the obvious, I was ecstatic and I also realized that in less than nine months, I was going to have the responsibility of a little being. And I blamed myself for not enjoying Emmanuel more before I got pregnant.

That evening he warned me that he would be home a little later. He had been asked to finish an urgent illustration at the very last minute. So I tried to pass the time by reading the brochure the doctor had given me. There were loads of things to think about, but I wasn't really into that. I still had some time ahead of me. If there was one night I could give him the candlelight dinner, this was it.

I bought what was needed to make a cheese soufflé. It was one of my most successful dishes. I went to the pastry shop to get a cake. The doctor had told me to avoid carrying heavy things, but it was still light.

When I got home, I started to prepare everything. My phone began to ring. It was John. We had last seen each other at a housewarming dinner party with a few close friends when I moved into Emmanuel's place. Since then, I hadn't heard much from him. Which was not look like John, with whom I was in contact at least once a week or more. But I was living in such a bubble of happiness with Emmanuel that it was kind of my fault. It was I who neglected my relationship with John. And then he saw Emmanuel every day at work so he heard from me, indirectly at least. I picked up.

"Hey John, how is it going?"

"Good? I thought I'd see how you are."

"Everything is fine, more than fine even."

"Still on your little cloud?"

"More than ever."

"Don't tell me he's already proposed? Not that I would be surprised from him, but still…"

"No. And then I think you would know if he had. He

might have even asked for your opinion on where and how to ask for my hand?"

"You know, we may work in the same company, but we don't see each other all the time. I only deal with him when I have graphics to get from him, 2-3 times a week."

"That's not bad. And then there is the coffee break, lunch: admit that you see my man every day..."

Well there you go, I admit it. In fact, we see each other very often. And he talks to me about you all the time. Besides, that's what I'm calling you. I don't really know how to handle the situation. You are my best friend so I will never betray your secrets, but I have the impression that Emmanuel is trying to get information from me that you are not giving him."

"Such as?"

"Your exes. If you're close to them. Or what it is you prefer. So I'm trying to tell him he'd better ask you directly. In fact, since you've entered his life, we only talk about you. Not that I have a problem with the subject honey, but I feel like I lost my mate from work. All he cares about is knowing all about you."

"You're jealous, aren't you?"

"Me, jealous? That you fuck a guy with such a nice little ass? Yes !"

"Hands off, he's mine!"

"I saw him before you!"

"Yes, but he's mine!"

"Anyway, I'm not into straight nor bisexual men."

"Because Matthias was never bisexual?"

"Yes, but you know it's different. He's a repentant. Anyway, I'm trying to make Emmanuel understand that it would be good if we resumed our conversations from before. When we were laughing at everything and nothing... But when I point it out to him, he tells me that we have the most awesome person in the world in common and that he wants to know everything about you.

And who else than his best friend to teach him everything?"

"But when we're together, I feel like we already spend our time telling each other about our lives. He just has to ask me his questions directly..."

"That's what I'm trying to tell him! But it always comes down to you. It bothers me to ask you to mediate so that he understands that I would like it to be the same as before you met..."

"Don't worry, I'll tell him about it, but maybe not tonight, because I have something important to say myself."

He paused…

"Are you pregnant?"

"How do you know?"

It had come out on its own. I had just announced to my best friend that I was pregnant before even confirming it to the man in my life. There was a blank on the other end of the phone.

"I didn't tell you anything. Pretend you don't know if Emmanuel announces it to you tomorrow."

"Since when have you been pregnant?"

"It's been a month."

Silence at the other end of the line. I heard the key in the lock on the entrance door.

"I gotta hang up, Emmanuel is coming. Talk to you later!"

I quickly hung up and put the receiver back as Emmanuel walked through the front door. I threw myself into his arms before kissing him languidly. He pulled away from my lips. My heart was pounding at two hundred an hour, I was so nervous.

"So are you?"

"Yes!"

He lifted me up and spun me in the air while kissing me with incredible passion.

"You couldn't make me happier…"

"Are you sure?"

"Do you doubt it?"

"I'll admit that a part of me is still afraid that you will grab your stuff and run away."

"Well, you already live at my place so that would be complicated and above all, you give me the best news: I'm going to be a dad! How do you want me to run away when you're the prettiest mum?"

What a charmer!

"Yeah, we'll see in a few months if you still find me so pretty when I look like a whale."

"To me you will always be the most beautiful, my little princess."

"You will see that you will say the same to your daughter."

"Do you think it will be a girl?"

"At this point, I don't know. I think we only know after a few months…"

"It would be so good to have a little girl who has your eyes…"

"Or a little boy who looks like you…"

"I absolutely have to tell my mother, she's going to be overjoyed!"

"Certainly not! You have to wait for the first ultrasound in two and a half months. The doctor said there was a risk of miscarriage until then. And first of all, I don't even know your parents. Maybe you should introduce them to me before you tell them the news!"

"You're right. I'll call them to see if we can go to Le Tréport this weekend. But I think I would like to celebrate this first!"

"If your intention is to open the champagne, it's going to be difficult now that I'm pregnant."

He took me in his arms and carried me to bed.

"I was thinking about something else…"

Twenty minutes later, the smell of burnt soufflé dragged us from our carnal celebration. Emmanuel prevented me from taking care of it. He didn't want our baby to smell something burnt. He told me to stay at the window to breathe fresh air and ordered pizza. Which left us thirty more minutes to pick up where we left off.

Just before the delivery man arrived, Emmanuel was lying on his side close to me stroking my stomach. Nothing could yet be discerned of the unborn baby. I thought aloud to myself:

"It's still crazy that it arrived so quickly, isn't it?"

"Yes. The ways of the Lord are impenetrable…"

What? I was a little surprised that he said that, but I didn't have time to pick up on it because the intercom was ringing. It was the delivery guy. Emmanuel got up and put on a dressing gown. He came back two minutes later with the pizzas and asked me if I wanted to eat in bed... I was so hungry and lazy to move that I greeted his proposal with enthusiasm. I didn't think any more about this religious remark that Emmanuel had made.

Not at all, until the following weekend when I was able to finally meet his parents for the first time...

CHAPTER 6
ORDEAL BY PARENTS

You should never give birth to the child of a man without knowing his parents... Let's say if I had met Emmanuel's parents before, I would have thought twice before making one with him.

We arrived in Normandy on Saturday late morning. Emmanuel gave me a great picture of his family: four brothers and sisters, a lawyer father, a stay-at-home mother. I understood better, moreover, why he wanted so much to have children: he came from a practicing Catholic family with many siblings. The brainwashing must have started in childhood.

I couldn't help but think back to the Monty Python's sketch in *The Meaning of Life* where a Catholic father tells in a room full of his offspring of all ages that every drop of sperm is sacred and should only be used for procreate.

His brother, Paul, who had been at school with John was to be there too with his wife and two children. He painted me a picture of a happy family. Not being a Catholic, I had worried if his family would take it badly, but he reassured me by telling me that they were open.

John's mother had never worked and I wondered how she was spending her days now that all of her children were gone while her husband was still active. When we arrived, she was mowing the lawn in the garden adjoining the house: everything was perfect, a bit like the French gardens of Versailles. Trees were pruned into square or round shapes, flower beds were arranged in symmetrical shapes. Even the vegetable garden was perfectly maintained. Marie-Bénédicte, Emmanuel's mother, looked funny when she saw me, as if she was disappointed. She came to meet and greet us.

"Hello, excuse my outfit, I wanted to finish mowing the lawn before you got there."

"No worries mum. Let me introduce you to Julia. Julia, this is my mother, Marie-Bénédicte."

"Nice to meet you, I replied, holding out my hand."

She took off her gardening glove to give it an energetic squeeze, then kissed her son on the cheeks.

"I'll finish mowing. I need another five minutes. Your father is in the kitchen, he insisted on preparing the leg of lamb. He should be in the kitchen. Your brother is coming in half an hour."

"Ok, we're going to go help Daddy then. See you later."

I waited until I was out of Marie-Bénédicte's reach to speak with Emmanuel. I wanted to share my concern with him because when she saw me, her mother had displayed a crestfallen face. Emmanuel pushed open the door of the house and entered. It was a typical Norman half-timbered house. The exposed beams of the ceiling gave it an old and rustic charm. I had never set foot in a house like this.

"Is this where you lived all your childhood?" I said.

"Yes."

"It's magnificent."

"I find the style a bit dated, but that's how all the houses in the area were before."

"I find it very beautiful. Hey, your mum looked at me weirdly when we arrived, is that normal?"

"But what are you saying? I'm sure she adores you already!"

Emmanuel had the gift of reassuring me, but in his attitude there was something strange. He took me in his arms and kissed my forehead. Emmanuel's father appeared in the doorway to the kitchen.

"Ah there you are! With all the uproar your mum is making, I wasn't sure if you had arrived. Don't stay there, come in!"

Emmanuel took my coat and hung it on a hook as his father walked over to shake my hand. He was wearing an apron and looked so much like Emmanuel, but with wrinkles and white hair. If Emmanuel turned out like his father over the years, I didn't have to worry... He held out his hand:

"Hello Lucie."

Emmanuel corrected him:

"Her name is Julia, Daddy."

"Julia, of course! Am I stupid! It's just that you look so much like her! Lucie was Emmanuel's former girlfriend."

Emmanuel was indignant:

"Daddy!"

Emmanuel had never told me that I looked like his ex. Perhaps that explained his mother's gaze earlier. I was starting to build scenarios in my head. Was it possible that Emmanuel chose me for just that reason and went about it so quickly with me because I reminded him of his ex? Did he want to go further with me where he hadn't been able to with her? Or did he just have a specific type of girl? His father drove the point home:

"Well, it's true Emmanuel, they could be sisters."

He stared at him to make him stop. Damn, I knew it! It was too good to be true. My Prince Charming had suddenly transformed into Bluebeard who collected women and killed them one after the other. And I was pregnant with his child! Help! Emmanuel asked:

"Can we help you with anything?"

"No, everything's ready. The leg is roasting."

I already imagined a human-sized oven in which I would be put in alive once I gave birth. Or even before!

"On the other hand, we can set the table together if

that's ok with you," his father urged us.

He turned and I glanced at Emmanuel who for the first time avoided my gaze and pretended to stare at his father. I envisioned the worst. I suddenly felt bad.

"Barthélémy, can I ask you for a glass of water, please? I asked Emmanuel's father."

"But of course, come to the kitchen, I'll give you one right away."

The kitchen was just as rustic as the rest of the house. Old copper pans hung on the wall.

"There you go, JULIA", he said while handing me the glass.

He had emphasized on my name, as if to show me that he wanted to get over his previous blunder. This only made my uneasiness worse.

I would have drunk the water all at once, but I didn't want to come across as being rude and drank slowly. I felt a little better, but my doubts were circling in my head. His father opened a door:

"Follow me, we'll set the table."

In the dining room, he opened the dresser and held up the porcelain he passed to us for us to lay out on the table.

I was setting the cutlery while Emmanuel arranged the plates. Barthélémy was busy getting the glasses out.

"What do you do for a living, Julia?"

"I'm a project manager in an agency that creates websites."

"And in actual fact, what do you do with your days?"

"I make sure that the websites correspond to the client's wishes from A to Z. I coordinate all the stakeholders so that the project is delivered on the launch date desired by the client."

"You're a bit like a site manager."

"Except it's virtual."

"And do you enjoy it?"

"Yes, a lot."

"You could work together with Emmanuel if you so wished…"

"Yes, he could always create the graphic identity for one of our clients.

"And you don't use his services?"

"No, we already have graphic designers working for us internally and Emmanuel has got more than his share of work where he is."

"Maybe it's best after all. Working together as a couple is not always a good idea..."

"Why? Did you work with your wife?"

"No, but we already can't cook together without it ending in a fist fight so I can't even imagine what it would be like at work…"

I was surprised that he told us this kind of confidence, but Emmanuel laughed at this remark. So it had to be a well-known fact in the family. The front door creaked and made me jump. I turned around. Footsteps were getting closer. I recognized Marie-Bénédicte's voice:

"Emmanuel, Barthélémy, where are you?"

"In the dining room, Mum!"

"But what are you doing Barthélémy, you're making them set the table?"

"Honey, they were keen to help, I was not going to let all this goodwill go to waste", said Barthélemy.

I still felt bad.

"Could you show me where the bathroom is, please?"

"Yes, of course, follow me."

Marie-Bénédicte led me back to the entrance and pointed to a door at the end of an adjacent hallway. That Barthélémy called me by Emmanuel's ex's name didn't please me at all, let alone hearing that she looked just like me. As for Marie-Bénédicte, she had stared at me so strangely... I felt out of place here and I had a bad feeling. I looked at myself in the mirror over the basin. I wondered in which way Lucie and I looked alike. I had never seen a photo of her. I was going to have to investigate on the Internet when I got home.

Emmanuel had told me about this ex with whom he had been for two years. She was the one who left him. He had had a hard time getting over it. The reason had struck me as a little obscure. She had told him that she was no longer in love with him... I had asked Emmanuel if she had met another man, but he had told me no, although a few months later he had discovered that she had found someone else. They hadn't been together for nearly a year now, but she was the last girl her parents had known and obviously loved. A little too much for my taste... I took a deep breath and walked back to the living room. Bartholomew exclaimed:

"Ah, there you are, we were about to uncork the champagne!"

"I will be fine with water."

"Come on Julia, this is the first time we've met, we're going to celebrate!"

"I'm sorry, but I only drink on very rare occasions."

Marie-Bénédicte exclaimed:

"That's not what Emmanuel told us! It seems that the whole village is aware of your monumental carousal on the evening of the PSG-Caen match."

I looked at Emmanuel furiously! How could he have told them that?

"Well, that taught me a lesson, I haven't had a drop since!"

"Really?" asked the Father Inquisitor, slightly suspicious.

Emmanuel came to my rescue.

"Leave her alone, if she doesn't feel like drinking alcohol, you shouldn't force her."

Marie-Bénédicte looked at me questioningly.

"You wouldn't be pregnant by any chance?"

At these words, I turned pale. We had agreed with

Emmanuel that no matter what, nothing should be said about my condition until the first ultrasound.

"We didn't want to say anything for the moment, but yes... Julia is pregnant."

I went pale, but not as much as Emmanuel's mother.

"What?", she exclaimed.

"She is just over a month pregnant," replied Emmanuel proudly.

I was expecting congratulations... Anything, except the response of Marie-Bénédicte...

"What went through your mind Emmanuel? You bring us home a girl who is not even a Catholic when Lucie was. And you get her pregnant before you even get married?"

Was I invisible for her or what? Now I understood. I had fallen into a nest of hard-line Catholics. All of a sudden I understood the unease in the air better. Barthélémy made things worse:

"Emmanuel, things are done in order. What got into you? You barely know each other."

"We know each other well enough to know that we want to make our life together."

The Mother Superior was annoyed:

"Okay, but in this case, get married before the child is born."

They all spoke as if I was not there. It was time for it to stop:

"I'm not really in favour of marriage."

It was as if I had said a bad word. The Father Inquisitor and the Mother Superior turned together.

"What?"

"I mean... I'm not completely against it and if it is important to Emmanuel, I would marry him, but for me it is not essential. It's just a piece of paper."

"A paper?!"

Emmanuel's mother looked like she was on the verge

of fainting. She repeated incredulously:

"A paper? Do you realize what she just said, Barthélémy?"

The Father Inquisitor went on:

"Julia, marriage is more than a piece of paper. It is an act of love before God."

"Or just a paper to sign at the Town Hall that says two people decide to get together to pay lower taxes. I'm not baptized anyway so I don't think I can get married in church."

Marie-Bénédicte put her hand to her heart and had to sit down. Emmanuel looked at me as if to say: "Don't add any more, please...". I frowned for him to read in my eyes, "I do what I want and if you're not happy you get out!".

The doorbell was heard ringing several times and the door opened. It was Emmanuel's older brother who had been to school with John. A little boy entered followed by his sister, a young woman obviously a few months pregnant, and a man who looked as Emmanuel as two drops of water, but slightly less cute. I had hit the jackpot in the family. The two children threw themselves into Emmanuel's arms.

"Uncle Manu!", said the little boy. "Let's play hide and seek!".

"Let your uncle breathe Baptiste", said Emmanuel's brother. "And you too Marie. Instead, say hello to Grandpa, Grandma and Julia."

Baptiste looked at me with big eyes.

"Is that you, Julia?"

"Yes."

He held out his hand to me, which seemed unnaturally well-behaved for a little boy this age. I was more used to children who did not want to greet and hid in their mother's skirts...

"Nice to meet you, Baptiste."

"You look just like Lucie..."

The truth comes from the mouths of children, they say. I looked at Emmanuel who began to stare at his feet, visibly embarrassed. Marie walked over to shake my hand while Baptiste went to kiss his grandparents. A distance could be felt between the grandchildren and the grandparents. These people were obviously not very demonstrative. Paul, Emmanuel's brother, did kiss me on both cheeks.

"They must be excused. I'm Paul and this is my wife Audrey."

"Delighted to meet you all."

I kissed Audrey on both cheeks as everyone finished saying hello to one another. Emmanuel whispered to me:

"Are you ok? I'm sorry for earlier. My parents loved my ex very much and for them religion is super important."

He took my hand and I felt a little tension dissipate. Emmanuel knew how to allay all my fears. Most importantly, he made me understand that he loved me, atheist though I was. Even though I was a little angry with him for not telling me about the situation or even my resemblance to Lucie. On second thoughts, I remembered now that we had talked about the marriage one night and when I told him my opinion of it, he had turned a little pale.

It was the first time I had heard a man talk about it anyway. Everyone else ran away at the mention of the word "commitment" in any form. He also asked me if I had a religion. I told him that I was an atheist and that for me religions were responsible for many more wars than good things in the world.

Now that I thought about it, he had raised his eyebrows at my response, saying that he had been brought up in the Catholic tradition, but that he was not practicing. Maybe he had been too anxious to please me and had dodged this little detail about his family, seeing that I was no more interested in the subject than that.

I also remembered now that sentence he had said: "*The ways of the Lord are unsearchable.*" I should have realized then that he was perhaps much more steeped in religion than I had suspected.

I wondered if Paul and Audrey would be nicer to me. After all, his brother had studied with John. He must have known he was gay. John had come out years ago, but I preferred not to mention the subject. I didn't want to appear doubly heretical to this family. But this time, it was Paul's turn to put his foot in it. As if he had read my mind...

"So apparently you're a good friend of John Langlois?"
"Yes, he's my best friend." I answered.
Marie-Bénédicte cried:
"The homosexual?"

Damn, she knew about it and I had just said, not only that he was a friend, but my best friend. I couldn't help but notice the look of disgust and disdain with which she had said "homosexual" and I felt the anger rising in me:

"Do you have a problem with homosexuality?"
"Yes, it bothers me: I think it is against nature and completely reprehensible. I hope you don't intend your child to see John after birth?"

It was starting to amuse me to infuriate the Mother Superior. I decided to continue to attack.

"Actually, I haven't told you about it yet, Emmanuel, I said, turning to him, but I was going to ask him to be our child's godfather."

Julia: 1–Marie-Bénédicte: 0: judging by Marie-Bénédicte's shocked look. I now knew that I had linked my destiny with my in-laws before I knew them and that they were certainly not going to turn me into a saint or change my beliefs. Now that I was carrying Emmanuel's child, it was too late to back down.

In any case, Emmanuel's parents lived in Le Tréport

and we had only been there once in a month of shared history. I was hoping that Emmanuel was not too much like daddy and that we would go as little as possible afterwards. At worst, I could always go to sleep at John's place and only call on his parents for official occasions. Audrey came out of the bathroom with Baptiste.

"Sorry, I think I skipped an episode. Are you pregnant Julia?"

I looked at her and then I looked at Emmanuel, not knowing what to say. He spoke.

"Yes, we didn't want to say anything until the first ultrasound, but Julia is a month pregnant."

"But that's fantastic! Congratulations to you both!"

Audrey kissed me on both cheeks. Finally one that had a normal reaction! She pointed her index finger in the direction of her round stomach.

"That's great, we will make them playmates!"

"Yes, for sure! When is yours due?"

"In five months!"

Paul tapped his brother on the shoulder.

"Well, Manu, you haven't wasted time!"

Emmanuel seemed visibly troubled to be under the onslaught of these questions. Barthélémy interrupted this moment of embarrassment.

"I think it's time to sit down and have lunch."

The children were the only ones to utter "yeah!". All this conversation had cut my appetite: not really normal for a pregnant woman. I had no idea how this lunch was going to be, but it couldn't be worse than these preliminaries. Unless it turned into a sermon on religion or worse, that no one uttered a word.

Deep down I knew the solution: I was only going to talk to children and ask them lots of questions. At least the conversation wouldn't be centered on our couple, the baby, or me.

Marie-Bénédicte designated the seating for each of us.

The women were all on one side and the men on the other. The Mother Superior had pointed out a chair for me to her left. So I found myself trapped between her and my "sister-in-law". I just hoped that Audrey would stop asking questions about my pregnancy and that Marie was going to give her full attention to eating. Fortunately, Marie-Bénédicte in her great kindness had put me facing Emmanuel: I was going to need him to face the worst lunch of my life. I could always fake nausea to slip away now that everyone was aware of my condition.

The problem is, since I had never had a child, I wondered if this lie could pass two women who had been there before. It was Marie-Bénédicte who launched the hostilities again while her husband went to get the first dish.

"And what do your parents do, Julia?"

"My father is a painter and my mother is an English teacher."

She must have judged that it was most certainly my artist father who must have instilled these pagan principles in me.

"And does he live off his art, your father?"

"Yes, pretty well. He remarried and settled in a loft in New-York with his wife who's a sculptor.

She rolled her eyes as if to say, "And he's divorced!"

"And your parents didn't get you baptized?"

"No, they gave me the choice. My father was a Protestant and my mother a Catholic. I went to Sunday school for a bit, but I quickly quit."

I wanted to avoid saying why. She didn't have to know that I was asking the priest disturbing questions every five minutes and that he had asked my parents to withdraw me from Sunday school as if I were the antichrist.

However, I forgot about my super tactic to stop the interrogation and asked the children point blank:

"So how old are you, Baptiste?"

"I'm four and a half."

"What about you Marie?"

"I'm two and one quarter."

"That's very precise... And what do you like to do after school?"

"To draw!"

My respite was only short-lived since Barthélémy arrived with a platter of foie gras and toasted bread. As luck would have it, I hate foie gras and couldn't suppress an expression of disgust when I saw the dish. Nothing escaped Marie-Bénédicte.

"Don't you like it, Julia?"

"Yes, yes. Normally, I love it, but now, I don't know why, it makes me gag."

Audrey came to my rescue:

"Yes, I have the same thing with some foodstuffs. Besides just yesterday, I couldn't touch the spinach that I had cooked for the kids and me. You couldn't say that I set a good example. Fortunately Paul was hungry enough for two..."

Audrey smiled lovingly at Paul.

"Anyway, if you don't want it, I'll gladly take your portion," she said.

Baptiste wasn't very happy and said:

"No! Me, me!"

Marie also said:

"No, it's mine!"

Emmanuel could not suppress himself:

"No, it's mine!"

Suddenly, I burst out laughing for the first time since I had entered that damn house. Barthélémy decided.

"We will cut in four, so no one is jealous."

I barely escaped foie gras. Anyway, my appetite still hadn't returned. Barthélémy began to serve the wine to the adults. Obviously, he had forgotten that I was pregnant, since he was about to pour some to me. I put a hand on the glass to prevent him.

"Oh, it's true sorry, I had forgotten. I'm going to get you some water."

I didn't have much to do except wait for the next course. If I let the Mother Superior place one word, I suspected that she would return tirelessly to matters that would annoy me. Baptiste dropped a piece of bread and foie gras on the floor.

"Oh no!"

"Pick it up, but don't eat it, Baptiste. What fell to the ground is dirty."

"But why?"

"We don't eat it, that's all! On the floor, it's not clean."

Baptiste picked up his piece of bread and foie gras, visibly disgusted at having to leave it. He put it back on the end of his plate. Paul asked his brother:

"So how's your new job going?"

"Very well. It was thanks to him that I found John and he introduced me to Julia."

Marie-Bénédicte was dismayed at these words. Part of her still must have hoped that the child wouldn't be born and that she could convince him to leave me for a good little Catholic like his ex.

"And what does John do in your company?"

"He's Marketing Director."

"I never thought he would do that for a living. It seemed to me he would become a writer or a journalist. He always had full marks in composition: the French teacher loved him. He wrote poems too..."

I almost spat back into my glass of water at these words. If John wrote poems, he never told me.

"He writes more newsletters or advertising campaigns than poems nowadays," I said.

John had never spoken to me about his literary inclination. I decided to dig into the subject later.

"When were you in class together?" I asked.

"From primary to second. It's a shame, I never saw him again. I wish I knew what happened to him..."

"It's too bad he's not here this weekend."

Paul's eyes widened.

"What do you mean?

"He bought a cottage here some time ago. Otherwise if you come to Paris one day, you can see him…"

"Paris, are you serious?"

He had said that earnestly, then the two brothers had burst out laughing. I was wondering why. Emmanuel continued.

"One of these days when you'll come to Le Tréport, we'll try to fix it."

"Does John often comes here?" asked Paul.

"Yes, every other weekend."

"You too are going to come often now."

I looked at Emmanuel, hoping he would say that Parisian life was too busy and that we would only come once in a while... as rarely as possible!

"Ah, you know my dream has always been to come back and live here. If only work allowed me..."

Ouch. Another thing we had never talked about together. Frankly, I hadn't even thought about whether he was homesick. I was swimming in the middle of a nightmare. I could already see myself living in this house with Barthélémy reading passages from the Bible to try and convert me, a baby bawling and Marie-Bénédicte running after me with a pitcher of holy water to baptize the child. Emmanuel resumed.

"Anyway, it's not up to me just now."

He had looked at me with a glimmer of hope in his eyes. What? No desire to spend anything other than weekends at Le Tréport!

"I doubt if I can find a job around here, I answered laconically so as not to give him false hope."

Marie-Bénédicte attacked again.

"Because you don't plan to stop working to raise your children?"

Decidedly, she did not let go. She had said it as if it was not possible for a second to leave the education of children to other people.

"Er, no."

Emmanuel came to my rescue.

"You know mum, in Paris it's almost impossible to survive without two wages."

"In Paris yes, but what about here?"

No, but she wasn't going to decide my life, Mother Superior, either! Who did she think she was? I couldn't believe how this conversation was going. I felt like I was undergoing a long litany of surrealist statements dating from a recent, but bygone era.

"It's not just a question of salary. I am not going to give up my career for my children."

"But still, there is nothing more important than children. Are you going to leave it to other people to take care of them?"

"But that's what all women do these days, I don't see what the problem is. Emmanuel can take care of the child full time if he prefers."

"But you can't leave this to a man. It's not his job to take care of the children."

"And why not?"

Years of feminism and we were still there? My question was left open. It was too much for me. I had to get out of this room.

"Would you please excuse me."

Emmanuel got up from the table and followed me. I told him once the door to the dining room was closed:

"Do you intend to come with me to the bathroom?"

"No, I just wanted to apologize for my mother's attitude."

"Well, don't worry, she can say whatever she wants, I

am as I am, take it or leave it."

"I love you as you are. Don't change a thing."

He kissed me. It made me forget for a brief moment the tension that this verbal fight had created.

I was not sure of what I had just said to Emmanuel. I wished he didn't love Normandy so much and could stay away from his family forever. When I returned, my plate had just been served.

I sat down and waited patiently for Marie-Bénédicte to bring the fork to her mouth so I could do the same. It would have been inappropriate to start eating before the hostess. My appetite had returned in the meantime. Barthélémy had put on a great spread. His leg of lamb was really excellent. How was it possible that Marie-Bénédicte left him in the kitchen since, according to her, children were exclusively women's business?

"It's really delicious Barthélémy", I said.

He smiled at me.

"Thanks. But I have nothing to do with it. We have an excellent butcher here."

Emmanuel sighed.

"Daddy, stop being modest, it's perfect."

I didn't want Marie-Bénédicte to attack again, so I took the lead of the conversation once more:

"Do you often cook?"

"Unfortunately no, work does not leave me the time to prepare good meals very often. Unfortunately, I come home too late at night, but I try to make up for it on weekends."

"Did you take lessons?"

"No, my mother taught me. And books too."

"You are really gifted!"

Barthélémy was definitely struggling with compliments. Even if Marie-Bénédicte was the worst harpy, if it meant eating five star food, I could consider reconciling myself with this family. Audrey continued:

"Emmanuel told us you had moved in with him?"

"Yes, my flat was too small for two, but anyway, since we're going to be three, we're going to have to start looking for something bigger."

"Are you going to buy or to rent?"

"To be honest, we were waiting to be a little more sure about the baby because that makes a lot of changes all at once."

Barthélémy asked if I wanted some more meat.

"Yes, please", I answered.

"I think it is better that you buy", he said. "Given the price of renting in Paris. And then at least it will be your place."

"Yes, we need to think about it. Everything went so fast..."

Paul patted his brother on the shoulder.

"Was it love at first sight between you two? How did you meet?"

"Through John. We saw each other on Dad's birthday. You had already returned to Dijon. And then we saw each other in Paris the next day. Here."

Marie-Bénédicte must have been calculating the dates in her head and deducing how easy a girl I was... Well, technically, I hadn't slept with him on the first night. Only the second...

I focused on the similarities between the two brothers and the father. It was funny to see those three faces and compare them to Baptiste in miniature.

In fact, all the men in this family looked disturbingly alike. As for Marie, she looked like her father and mother but had nothing of her grandmother. Phew. I was hoping that Emmanuel had not passed anything on from his mother to our daughter, if there was one. However, I wouldn't mind at all if my son looked like Emmanuel.

I was only beginning to realize that in just under eight months our child would be here. A little being who was going to have to be loved, nurtured and protected. Before, I don't think I really realized the responsibility that involved.

In fact, the only time I had any real difficulty was when I babysat a couple's baby while he had an ear infection. He hadn't stopped screaming for three hours and I had tried everything to calm him down, but nothing had helped. My eardrums still remembered it. Except it wasn't mine and I gave him back to his parents relieved and telling myself that I wouldn't be doing that again anytime soon. I was 23 at the time... A lot had changed since then. I was going to have to be there for my child no matter what when I didn't even feel him moving in my belly yet.

The plates were cleared and I got up to take the dish of lamb to the kitchen. Emmanuel took it from me.

"Do you remember the doctor saying you shouldn't carry anything heavy?"

"Yes, but this is almost empty and it's not heavy at all."

"Hop, hop, hop."

I sighed. Emmanuel was starting to be heavier than the tray. He joined his parents in the kitchen, leaving me alone with the children, Paul and Audrey.

"Don't mind my mum, Julia," Paul said. "She has super strict principles, but you just have to ignore her. She makes life difficult for everyone outside the family. No one is ever perfect enough for her. "

"Isn't that special treatment then?"

"No", said Audrey. Me too, she lectured me because I had returned to work instead of raising my children. At the moment, she's loosening my grip a bit because I took two years of maternity leave to take care of the children and the unborn baby..."

Barthélémy arrived with a tray of apple sorbets. It was time for the Norman hole... The children were delighted. Emmanuel arrived with the calvados in one hand and a salad bowl in the other while Marie-Bénédicte brought a cheese platter. He put the salad bowl down and started serving calva to all the adults except Audrey, the children and me. He whispered in my ear.

"Sorry sweetie, I know how much you love it!"

Decidedly, I couldn't believe that Emmanuel had told this story of drunkenness to his parents and that the whole village knew about it... Finally, I was really going to be able to keep my promise not to touch up a drop of alcohol at least for the next few months.

I felt that my body expressed only disgust at the idea of drinking even a drop, so I didn't have to force myself. It was like my body was telling me what to eat. It was very strange: I felt like I was possessed by an alien who was transmitting orders to my stomach. Anyway, he didn't seem to be saying no to some apple ice cream...

It was eaten pretty quickly, not to say devoured, then the cheese board began to be passed around the table. The children didn't like it too much, but their parents and especially their grandparents forced them to take a small piece of each kind to at least taste it. This injunction did not have too much effect on Marie, who had put a small piece of *Bleu d'Auvergne* on her tongue and immediately spat it out on her plate with a disgusted expression. This inspired the Mother Superior with a whole sermon on good manners. You had to learn to eat everything. Lots of hungry people dreamed of eating cheese right now, etc.

Marie began to cry not knowing what to do and I had a glimpse of the education Emmanuel and Paul had received. Of course, when dessert arrived, there were no more questions about having to eat it all. Marie and Baptiste threw themselves greedily on the chocolate *soufflé* their grandfather had prepared, accompanied by homemade whipped cream which they ate in one mouthful, just like me.

Marie-Bénédicte's assaults had finally ceased and the

conversation turned to the latest local events, including the regatta that was to take place the next day. We were to leave on Sunday afternoon, but luckily John had left us the key to his cottage. That lunch with my in-laws had been enough for me.

After promising to meet for the regatta the next day, it was time to say goodbye. We wanted to go to John's and do some shopping for the weekend. As I walked towards Emmanuel's car, I finally felt free.

"I think your mother was disappointed that we weren't staying at her place all weekend. Didn't you tell her we were going to John's?"

"No, I forgot. It's so obvious for her that I'm coming home when I'm in Normandy…"

"I'm relieved not to have to put up with your mum all weekend."

"Was it that horrible?"

"You witnessed the conversation yourself… First your father calls me the name of your ex, then the news that I'm pregnant… Besides, thank you for telling our secret in five minutes while you promised me not to say anything..."

He looked at me sheepishly.

"Not to mention their outrage over the marriage and everything ... How did your exes put up with all this?"

"I've only introduced them to one before you."

"And why did your father call me Lucie?"

"I have no idea."

"I have the impression he did it on purpose."

"He loved Lucie a lot. It was a shock when I told them that we had separated."

"You never told me she looked like me. Remind me why she left you?"

"She wanted to go around the world, and I didn't. And above all she didn't love me anymore. Anyway, even if she appeared good when she was with my parents, she also fooled them a lot. She pretended to be a practicing Catholic even though she only went to church when she came on weekends here. And like you, I believe that if she had had a child, she would not have stopped working to raise him. "

"How is it that you stayed with Lucie for two years and didn't get married or have children?" I asked.

"I don't think I was ready at the time. Neither was she, by the way. She always wanted to go out, travel. With my instinct, for home, she must have felt that I was in the way of her plans. She went around the world as soon as she left me. I wasn't interested in that. I don't think the grass is greener elsewhere. And above all, I always had doubts. I wasn't really sure that she was the woman of my life. Whereas as soon as I saw you, I knew it right away."

"Do all your girlfriends look alike?"

He looked embarrassed.

"It seems that I do have a type of girl."

"Does that mean I have to beware because if you meet a woman who looks like me you're going to fall madly in love with her?"

"No, that means you're my type and I don't want anyone but you. In case you still don't know, you're the woman of my life and I love you."

"How can you be so sure?"

"I know it, that's all."

"Even if your parents always hate me?"

"This too shall pass."

Nothing was less sure.

"Do you want to postpone going to the supermarket?"

"No, now that we're here, let's go, then it will be done."

He hadn't forgotten to be gallant and held out his hand to help me out. I took the opportunity to throw myself into his arms and hug him. I couldn't get enough of the smell of his body. If it had only been up to me, I could have spent my time glued to him. I was aware, however, that this was certainly a very sociable behaviour in the dog kingdom, but quite asocial for mankind. So I just sniffed him, then decided with great difficulty to detach myself from his arms to go do those damn errands.

We hadn't been far apart during that lunch, but had I been able to take his hand while it lasted, I know the stress caused by his mother and her unending judgments would have probably dissipated. Emmanuel calmed me completely. I kept staring at him while we were shopping. I was so absorbed in his gestures and his face that I forgot to listen to what he was saying to me... He snapped his fingers in front of me.

"Julia, what are you thinking about?"

"You..."

"Well you better focus on what we eat tonight... How about a cider chicken?"

"It sounds great, never had it. On the other hand, cider for the baby is not great, is it?"

"You're right, I hadn't even thought about it. We can try the apple juice version if you want."

I was confident in his culinary abilities. The least I could say about him was that he had inherited his father's gift. It was simple, since we were together, he had only delighted me.

When we arrived at John's place, we needed to get closer after what I now called in my personal story "Ordeal by Parents". Emmanuel's gentleness made me forget this episode and I was just starting to enjoy this weekend at Le Tréport. While eating the apple juice chicken, a very honest conversation began. Now that I had met his family, I understood their values better and wanted to know more.

"Do you have a picture of Lucie on you?"

"No, I erased them all from my cell phone after we broke up, why?"

"I was just curious to know what she looked like."

"What's the use of seeing her? She looks like you, that's all. Either way, you shouldn't run into her, she's thousands of miles from here with her new boyfriend and she's now moved on."

"Are you sure you don't feel anything anymore for her?"

"Certain."

"But you stayed two years with her... It is often said that it takes as long to recover from someone as the number of years you have spent with that person."

"Julia, at the risk of repeating myself: I love you and I have never felt for anyone else what I feel for you."

He hugged me and said again:

"Not for anyone else."

"Sorry, the reaction of your parents and your nephew when they saw me scared me a little."

"Julia, you are much more beautiful, smarter and more fantastic than she is. And then, I already told you, as soon as I saw you and even before meeting you, I knew that you were the woman of my life. I felt like I had known you forever."

"I know. Me too. And why didn't you tell me that your parents were fundamentalist Catholics?"

"They're not fundamentalists!"

""Excuse me, but the mother who stays at home to look after her children, homosexuality against nature, a child who cannot be born out of wedlock, what do you call that?"

"I call it principles. Maybe a little retrograde, but you know I don't share them anyway. If you wanted to raise our child and stop working, I would support you, even if I think it's from another time. As for John, I wouldn't be friends with him if I shared my mother's opinion on homosexuality. Finally, as far as marriage is concerned, I don't want to force you if it only represents a paper for you."

"But it's important for you, isn't it?"

"Yes, but what matters the most is that we're together."

"Emmanuel, if that's what you want, I'll give you my hand. You told me that you might ask me for it again one day, remember..."

Emmanuel pulled me against him and hugged me. He whispered in my ear:

"I love you so much Julia."

I whispered to him in turn:

"Me too.

He ran his hand through my hair and kissed me.

"You also didn't tell me that all the men in your family look so alike."

"Ah, you think so?"

"Wait, this is striking! Your father is you older, your brother almost looks like he's your twin and your nephew looks like you in a small version."

Emmanuel started to laugh.

"What do your sisters look like?"

"Like my mother."

I burst out laughing.

"Do you think your mother and I will get on one day?"

"I don't know. My mother is very firm in her beliefs. Let's say that if you agree to get married before the birth of our child and have him baptized, she will surely always consider you an outcast, but you will at least have respected the sacraments of the Catholic Church. As for me, I would like our child to be baptized."

"But why? What difference does it make?"

"Well, you will go to hell and our child and I will go to paradise."

He had said it with humour, but I wasn't so sure he was really joking.

"I know that you find that religions put men against each other, he continued, but I think the opposite. Catholicism, whatever people say, gave me values of compassion, kindness and openness. And for me, it is very important.

"But one can have these values without believing in God."

"Yes, you're right. Besides, I couldn't have fallen madly in love with a girl who doesn't share them."

"You know, since we've been together, I find you so perfect, I kept searching what could be wrong about you. Now I know what it is."

"What is it?"

"Your family!"

CHAPTER 7
SEVEN MONTHS AND A HALF WITHOUT CLOUDS...

After this weekend with Emmanuel's family, I did everything to avoid going to Normandy. I had a good excuse: I had to limit my travel since I was pregnant. In fact, I could have travelled because it is only between six and nine months that a pregnancy is problematic, but Emmanuel did not know that and I certainly was not going to tell him. He was so considerate: he did the shopping, stopped me from cooking or cleaning and took care of everything without me being able to lift a finger.

I found his behaviour a bit excessive and resented that I couldn't do much when he was around. But in truth, it wasn't that bad to be cocooned for nine months before our child arrived, to take up most of our attention and sleep.

In comparison, meeting my mother had been a real pleasure. She had invited us to her apartment in Meaux and had been enchanted by Emmanuel. She had told me privately that she thought I had hit the jackpot.

When she heard the news I was pregnant, she shed a tear and hugged us. She couldn't believe she would soon be a grandmother.

We even called my father together via Skype to tell him the news. My parents had been apart for years and still remained on good terms. They had realized that they had become more friends than lovers and had mutually agreed to separate three years after I was born. My father had returned to the United States where he was from, leaving me and my older sister in my mother's care.

He promised to visit us in Paris in a month. He was to meet gallery owners there for his new works. He too was overjoyed. His new wife, Jenny, who had known me since I was little, was delighted too. My half-brother, William was at their house when we called. Suddenly, everyone had been informed or almost...

I hadn't spoken to my big sister since my return from Mexico and I had no desire for this child to be used as a pretext to reconcile us, even if my mother insisted. I turned a deaf ear.

Emmanuel therefore "saw" most of my family in one afternoon and he did not have to put up with my father, my stepmother or my half-brother for very long. My mother had decreed that she adored Emmanuel. She had already asked us to come see her as often as we wanted and immediately asked what she could offer the baby.

In the meantime, we still had one major problem to resolve: housing. We lived in Emmanuel's two-room apartment. However, we would now need an extra bedroom for the baby, or even two since we were planning to have two children.

I had always wanted to buy something in Paris, but with only one salary, I was doomed to only be able to buy a maid's room, or maybe an attic. Emmanuel also wanted to invest and had set aside a lot of money for this purpose. We were so confident in our relationship that it was easy for us to consider buying something together. The parental ordeal had finally brought us together.

Like everything since I had met Emmanuel, luck smiled upon us. We had looked for several apartments in the neighbourhoods we liked and as soon as we first saw this one we fell in love with it. It was a four-room apartment of 85 m2. The rooms were a bit small, but it had a lot of charm and was located in a typical Haussmann building. There was an old wrought iron elevator that still worked and the apartment had a tiny terrace.

It cost a small fortune of course and we would certainly take thirty years to pay it off, but given the Parisian rents, it would surely be cheaper than the rental equivalent. Our offer was accepted and a week later, an appointment was made with the notary.

That evening Emmanuel took me again to the restaurant where we had kissed for the first time. We were seated at the same table, I thought to celebrate this purchase. And when I wasn't expecting it at all, he dropped to one knee and pulled out a little box saying:

"Marry me Julia!"

It wasn't even a question. It was almost an order, but he had said it in such a sweet, irresistible way... I sat dumbfounded for a few seconds, not being able to believe what he was doing. He opened the case and a gold ring appeared.

I had never really thought about getting married before. For me, it had never been more than a contract... What had always mattered to me was to find a man whom I would love madly and with whom I would like to have children. It was the only commitment that had any real value to me. But this was the man of my life and the future father of my child who asked me to marry him and I knew how important it was to him. I heard myself say it almost automatically.

"OK".

He put the ring on my finger and just like our first date, he pulled me towards him and kissed me. This time, the people on the terrace applauded loudly. I didn't know where to put myself. Especially I suddenly wondered with horror when the ceremony would take place... I was going to look like a whale in my dress if we didn't do this very quickly... I whispered to him:

"But we have to get married quickly because I wouldn't want anyone to see that I'm pregnant in the photos."

"Don't worry. I'm taking care of everything".

This man kept surprising me! In the following month we were married. I was in my third month of pregnancy and I was able to cover it all up with a First Empire style dress. He had managed to convince the priest of Le Tréport church to perform the ceremony and he had arranged for my father to be present.

Only family members attended the marriage. My half-brother was my witness while Madeleine, Emmanuel's sister who lived in Lyon, was his. Usually I found wedding ceremonies long and tedious. But there, immersed in Emmanuel's eyes, the hour of the ceremony passed at breakneck speed.

When it was time to take the vows, I had pinched myself so much I felt like I was in a dream. This beautiful, caring and kind man, this fantastic lover, the future father of my child was what I had always dreamed of. And he wanted me, until death do us part! I wanted to cry with joy, to go up to the roof of the church to cry out to whoever wanted to hear it:

"He chose me!!!!!"

I still couldn't believe it. And when he put the ring on my finger and kissed me, a tear fell from my eyes, my emotion was so strong. This man, whose simple kiss sent me into the stratosphere, had amazed me all the way. If a seer had told me that in three months of dating I would be pregnant, married and soon to be a homeowner in Paris, I would have laughed at her.

Emmanuel wiped my tear away with his hand and said:

"Everything's going to be fine Mrs Julia Tellier".

I corrected him:

"Mrs Fletcher-Tellier."

Emmanuel smiled:

"As you wish my little wife."

He picked me up and kissed me again, overjoyed. I had

to tell him to avoid this while I was pregnant because it made me feel sick. But I was so happy to share his joy. He put me down while kissing me and said:

"You make me the happiest man on earth."

"And me the happiest woman."

Marie-Bénédicte must have been horrified that I was entering the family so soon, but she showed nothing of it and put on a good face all day. I was on cloud nine anyway.

It had been so long since I had seen my family reunited. And then I finally met Emmanuel's sisters, who indeed looked as alike as two drops of water and like their mother when she was younger. We had been to eat in an inn and then around 11 p.m. everyone had gone to bed. By the time I left, I was washed out.

We had booked a hotel room for the occasion. The fatigue suddenly disappeared when Emmanuel began to kiss me and undress me gently. My insatiable desire due to the pregnancy had a lot to do with the sleepless night that followed. Emmanuel had the gift of making me forget everything. Even fatigue. I fell asleep in his arms at dawn. We were crazy with happiness. Nothing could have clouded it.

CHAPTER 8
JUST A LITTLE DETAIL

Months had passed and we had moved into our new apartment. As usual, Emmanuel had everything planned. I hadn't even packed my own boxes. As soon as I offered to help him, he would tell me to enjoy, read a book, watch TV or sleep because lately I had become quite drowsy. It was lovely, but I was afraid he would burn out.

Fortunately, he let me give him a massage after a hard day of work. Emmanuel even went as far as to order professional cleaning after we moved in so that we did not have to dust. He still let me unpack the boxes the weekend we moved in, but whenever I tried to move something heavy, I always saw him come to my rescue. I had never seen someone so considerate. It was almost too much. I wasn't made of porcelain after all!

Everything was ready for the arrival of our little Clara since yes, it was a girl. Except that Emmanuel's father had been taken to the A&E room overnight from Friday to Saturday. Doctors had done a number of tests on him before declaring that he needed an investigation to see what he had.

I was eight and a half months pregnant and I was hardly delighted to see Emmanuel leave for his father's bedside when the birth was due at any moment.

Marie-Bénédicte had first called Emmanuel because he was the nearest. He had gone there in the night by car. Paul had taken the train the next morning. Madeleine, who lived in Lyon, had also gone. Even Eleonore, the youngest, who lived in London had taken the first

Eurostar to go to her father's bedside. Le Tréport was about two hours from Paris by car and I figured that if anything happened, I would call Emmanuel and he would have time to get home before I gave birth. Well, that was what I was hoping for...

I found it hard to imagine that a first child could arrive as predictably as a letter in the mail. When my girlfriends had their babies, the delivery had lasted between five and thirty-six hours. So I didn't think it would happen any faster, which would give Emmanuel plenty of time to come back.

So I took advantage of the weekend to relax and try to sleep. The exercise was made difficult by the weight of my belly, Clara's drumming and the news that Barthélémy had a tumour in his pancreas.

Of Emmanuel's two parents, his father was by far my favourite. Not only did he cook like a god, but he also tempered Marie-Bénédicte's ardour and protected me with kindness.

Although I never usually did, I prayed that he would survive. This family was definitely starting to rub off on me... John had also gone down with Matthias to Le Tréport for the weekend, so I was surprised when he called me on Sunday morning.

"Hello?"

"Hey Julia. I absolutely need to talk to you. Can I come in about... thirty minutes?"

"Yes, but I thought you were in Normandy..."

"I'm arriving in Paris. I will explain the situation."

His voice was infinitely sad. He sounded as though he was about to cry. I had never heard him in this state before. I sensed the worst. I decided to stop getting lost in guesswork and called Emmanuel to find out how things were going on his side.

"Are you in labour?" He asked immediately.

"No, don't worry, I just wanted to hear from you and

your father. How is he?"

"He is very weak. It hurts me to see him like that. I feel like he aged ten years since diagnosis. He's on a drip and they are giving him painkillers. But the operation went well, apparently they managed to remove the tumour."

"This is good news! And your mother, how is she holding up?"

"She cried yesterday in my arms. She has a panic fear of being alone without my father. You know, they've been together for thirty-five years and this is the first time she's realized he could die overnight. But he is off the hook it seems. He will have to be very well cared for to avoid relapses though."

"What about your brother and sisters, how are they taking it?"

"They are very distressed. We were really scared of losing my father during the operation. By the way, I saw Paul earlier who told me that he had seen John when he left the train station yesterday afternoon."

"It's weird. John just called me, he's already back in Paris. It's not his usual habit to come home so early on a Sunday morning when he's at Le Tréport for the weekend. He didn't want to tell me what it was about, but I have a feeling something bad happened. Maybe with Matthias? He should be here soon. I'll leave you to your family. Kiss them for me. What time do you think you'll be back in Paris?"

"I'll leave after lunch, probably around three o'clock to avoid traffic jams."

"Ok. I'm not moving anyway, it's not like I can..."

"I will be there very soon, don't worry."

"I love you."

"Me too. I can't wait to hold you in my arms."

"Not sure my waistline still allows you to right now..."

He laughed.

"See you later…"

I didn't have to wait for long before John rang at the door. He had the face of someone who hadn't slept at all. I had never seen him like this. I instinctively took him in my arms as much as I could with my big belly. He let me hold him.

"Matthias left me."

I was speechless for a moment.

"What? But why?"

"It's a long story."

"Si down first. Can I offer you a drink?"

"If you can make some coffee, that'd be great."

"It's on. Tell me everything."

"I don't know where to begin…"

I looked at him without understanding yet the magnitude of what he was about to tell me.

"I think I'm gonna start with the beginning. My first love is someone you know."

"What?"

"Yes, he's one of your new family."

I sat down, imagining the worst. I prayed that he would not tell me...

"Don't tell me it's Emmanuel."

"No!"

I sighed in relief. Even though it sounded crazy to me, I asked:

"His father?"

"Of course not!"

"One of Emmanuel's sisters?"

He stared at me impatiently. There was only one possibility left...

"Paul?"

He nodded.

"But that's impossible. He's heterosexual and has three children!"

"Precisely, you're right, it's impossible. That's what I said to myself throughout the journey to Paris. Our story is a bit like *Brokeback Mountain* set in Normandy. Except I turned serious gay and he turned repressed gay..."

I was so surprised by this revelation that I was speechless. Only the hiss of the coffee maker got me out of my torpor. I switched it off and made him a cup. John continued.

"I fell in love with Paul the first time I saw him. I was six years old."

"That young?"

"Yes. At that time, I didn't know what love at first sight was, let alone what homosexuality was. Anyway, from day one, I was irresistibly drawn to him and I felt that this little boy was going to be so much more than my friend, even though I didn't know how yet. We were the best friends in the world. We shared everything. Except that I realized that I was jealous. Where I refused all the advances of girls, Paul had lovers he kissed on the mouth. I looked at them and was dying to do the same with him, and it finally happened one rainy afternoon when we were playing together in his room. We were eleven. His hand brushed mine. I grabbed it. His face was very close to mine. I kissed him. He didn't push me away, quite the contrary. But I heard a noise in the stairs which ended the kiss. We didn't talk about it any more. After that, whenever we were alone, we would spend hours kissing, but these were forbidden hours. I was already aware of that at the time. We weren't talking about what was going on between us. It was taboo even for us and even more so for him. You saw his family, you know what I'm talking about..."

"Oh yes! I'm even surprised that you have gone so far with him without Catholic morals or his mother getting involved."

"Well years passed by. We slept very often at each other's place. And what was bound to happen happened one night when his parents were out and I was staying for a slumber party. It was a total ecstasy for me to have sex with him for the first time. I knew he was flirting with a girl back then: he told me it was to get his parents off his back and that deep down he only loved me. We stole all the moments we could. One day when we were at my house on a Wednesday afternoon, we did not hear my mother come home. She surprised us in bed. She had always known deep down that I was gay, but seeing me with Paul was a shock to her. She could not accept that my best friend, so good in all respects and so Catholic, was in fact my boyfriend. It was during this period that my father did everything he could to transfer to Paris and that I had to say goodbye to Le Tréport and to Paul. My father thought that my fondness for men would eventually disappear. I've never been so torn in my life. Of course, other than my parents, no one knew anything. I had begged my mother not to say anything to Paul's family. I have never forgotten him in all these years. My parents had sold the house and I could have gone back to see him, but my mother forbade me. I suppose she hoped that my homosexual inclination was only an adolescent phase and not a permanent state. And it was Paul who finally asked me after a few months to stop writing to him. He had met a girl and he was in love. What had happened between us was a youthful mistake, according to him."

"He must have been indoctrinated by his family."

"For sure! I always thought that he had convinced himself that he was really straight, but I never believed it. I know quite a few repressed homosexuals who have wives and children and who wake up at 40. They realize that they have done their duty and met the demands of their families, but they fall into depression because they have gone against their nature. Or they leave everything to go and live with a person of the same sex. In fact, I never told Matthias, but the reason I wanted to buy a cottage in Le Tréport was because I was hoping to run into Paul. I knew from friends that he came back there from time to time. And then one day, Emmanuel landed in my company. You saw how much he looks like his brother... When I saw him appear, I thought it was him."

"Don't tell me you wanted to try your way with him..."

"Well, I wouldn't have said no, but don't worry, there's nothing homosexual about him."

"Phew. But you must have asked him about his brother like crazy, right?"

"I tried to do this quietly. I knew he was married and had two children. Emmanuel told me that his wife was pregnant with the third. Part of me was disgusted: he had a family when I had always dreamed of having children with him. He was trying to fit. I supposed he must be bisexual now or that I was truly a youthful mistake. When Emmanuel came to visit us in Normandy, my crazy hope was that his brother would find out and that I could finally see him again. That was when Emmanuel saw your photo."

"Matthias knows that Paul is your childhood sweetheart?"

"No, I never told him anything. Until yesterday... I was going to get some bread and ran into Paul as he was leaving the train station, alone. He came to visit his father in the hospital. Seeing him, I knew nothing had changed. I hugged him like an old friend, but everything in me was screaming my love for him. Like when I was sixteen when I said goodbye to him for the last time. It was as if the past years hadn't erased anything. I offered to go for a coffee. I expected everything except what he told me then. He had never forgotten me. He had never made love to another man after me. His mother had read one of my letters and learned what had happened. It was she who had forced him to write to me, asking me to stop all correspondence. She had convinced him that he was heterosexual and seeing how much he had a choice, he started dating

Audrey, his best friend. He had convinced himself that he loved her, but never found with her what united us. Of course, Audrey doesn't know about anything."

I imagined Audrey's face if she were to learn this...

"I was stunned. I would have left Matthias on the spot if he had asked me to, but he didn't. He told me it was better to leave it as it is. That it was too complicated. We had little time and he had to go to his father's bedside. He took my phone number and promised to call me soon. I hugged him one last time like I was never going to see him again. We were in a public place and you know how they are in Le Tréport... Everyone knows everyone and everything is known very quickly so I didn't dare kiss him. His touch awakened feelings that I thought were buried forever and that I never thought I would have for anyone again. I realized that I could never love Matthias the same way, and when I got home, everything fell apart. I started to cry like when I was sixteen. Crying for all those lost years, for this love that I knew was there, but which would never be again. It was clear that Paul would not leave his wife or children. As for me, I could never love anyone else as much as him, you know?"

I nodded because I had never loved someone as much as Emmanuel. Weird this magnetism that these two brothers exert on us... He drank some of his coffee and continued.

"Seeing me in this state, Matthias asked me what was wrong. And I couldn't lie to him any longer. He understood right away that it was over, that there was nothing to add, that I would never love him as much as Paul. It took me years to say 'I love you' to Matthias and I think that's no accident. I couldn't tell him that the only person I ever loved was and always would be Paul."

"So he left?"

"Yes, last night. He needed to get away from me. He came back to our apartment in Paris."

"And you remained alone?"

"Yes. I couldn't sleep. And then Paul called me. He asked me if he could come round. I believe he sneaked away the night after your mother-in-law and Emmanuel came home from the hospital and went to bed. He arrived and we haven't exchanged a word. He kissed me and it was like before. I have had the best night of my life in years. It was as if I was coming back to life. I felt that all these years since we turned sixteen had been a parenthesis. That nothing was worth living outside of our love. We haven't slept all night. He left early morning."

"And you will meet again?"

"I don't know. I don't want to live without him, but I can't tear him away from his wife and children. In addition, Luc, their youngest, is only three months old. I don't want to destroy his family. Not to mention the reaction of his parents and Le Tréport if they found out that Paul was gay. It already took a while for people to stop looking at us askance, Matthias and me... Besides, I'm not sure it has completely stopped."

"But what did Paul say?"

"That he loved me. That he had never loved anyone other than me. But that coming out and leaving his wife and children was going to take superhuman courage that he wasn't sure he had."

"But he considered it. That's already a lot for a night of reunion."

"Yes, it's true. But I'm afraid I ditched Matthias for nothing. For a youthful love that will never return."

"How is Matthias?"

"I don't know, I don't dare go home. I don't even know how to organize my life now. We will certainly have to sell the cottage in Le Tréport and I'll have to find another place to sleep."

"You can stay here if you want. Besides, we're not really going to be there when I'm in the hospital giving birth..."

"I'll now go home to face Matthias and the reality of our breakup. We're going to have to completely reorganize our lives. I wonder if I'm not going to telework from Normandy for a while, and leave the Paris apartment to him."

I felt my baby move in my belly.

"Ooh, that kicks in there."

I was sensitive to Clara's every move. I wondered when the baby would finally come and I prayed that it would not be now because I wanted Emmanuel to be by my side...

"Can I look?" he asked.

"Are you sure you want to discover a huge belly with some kind of protruding foot mark in the middle? I assure you it can be traumatizing..."

"I couldn't be more traumatized today."

I lifted my t-shirt. Indeed, we could see Clara's protruding foot. John touched it with his finger.

"It's crazy, I never thought you could see her so clearly through the skin."

"Me neither. I thought I would have a nice round belly until the end like you see in the photos of pregnant women."

"Julia, I think I have to confess something else to you. Sit down."

I sat down, quite apprehensive given John's serious demeanour.

"Do you remember the weekend you met Emmanuel?"

"Do I remember? Yes, very well, well... Except after our calva evening, why?"

"You and I made love that night."

"WHAT!?"

I looked at him to see if he was laughing at me, but he was dead serious.

"Are you kidding there? Are you telling me that the

flashes I had of you naked in the shower with a hell of a hard-on, it wasn't all in my head?"

I leaned back in the couch and put my hand to my stomach. A violent contraction had just made itself felt.

"You're OK?"

"No. I'm in great pain."

"What can I do to help?"

"Nothing, I have to wait for it to pass."

He brought me a glass of water which I drank straight away. The evidence then jumped out at me.

"Did we do it without a condom?"

"Yes."

"But are you crazy? Why didn't you tell me?! If it turns out this child is yours!"

"There are chances…"

CHAPTER 9
THE END OF AMNESIA

Suddenly, I felt my waters break beneath me: I had just time to get up to avoid the carnage on the couch.

"Oh, no! Not that! Not now!"

John looked at me speechless: we would have to rush to the hospital.

"Can we take your car?" I asked.

"Of course!"

"I need to call Emmanuel right away."

I feverishly dialled his number. He replied immediately:

"This is it?"

"Yes, my waters broke. John is with me. He's going to take me to the hospital, but please leave now..."

"I'm leaving right away. Wait for me, I'll be there as soon as possible. John will take care of you in the meantime. Everything will be fine."

"Yes, but please hurry up!"

He must have heard that I was panicking. Yet his voice had remained calm to reassure me, but nothing could calm me down: in the light of this revelation, I was bordering on hysteria. If this child was John's baby, I didn't even dare to envision the tidal wave it would create in my life as well as having to reveal to Emmanuel that I had slept with my gay best friend the day before we met. The anger went up suddenly.

"How could you do this to me?! Let me carry your potential child and make me meet the man of my life in the process? Why didn't you tell me?!"

"Julia, calm down! We need to get to the hospital and quickly! We can have this conversation in the car, but I'm afraid it will stress you too much for the baby's arrival."

"You better tell me everything because I want to know exactly what went through your mind! I just have to change, I can't go like this."

"Do you need my help?"

"No, don't touch me!"

I had never spoken to him like that before. I was angry with him. Why had he lied to my face when we had had that drink together at *Le Café des Phares*? And how could he have kept his love affair with Emmanuel's brother from me all these years when I was supposed to be his best friend? I grabbed a skirt from the cupboard and rushed into the shower to rinse off before getting dressed. As we took the lift, he started telling me about what really happened that night:

"Do you remember we were completely drunk?"

"Yes. It's one of the only things I remember."

"I'm more alcohol resistant than you are so I was still standing. You on the other hand, you were in a bad state and I could not leave you like this. Matthias was also completely drunk and he went straight to bed. You asked me if I would do it with a girl and especially if I would do it with you. You then suggested that we make a baby together."

I had to lean on the bonnet of the car because of another contraction that finally passed a minute later. He opened the door for me and helped me sit up, placing his arm behind my back, then we left very quickly. Despite the panic, I harassed John to spit everything out. He tried to keep going while keeping his attention on the road.

"Just before that afternoon, we brought up the issue of children again with Matthias. It was even I who suggested to him that we could ask you to be the mother. He saw red and he thought I wanted to do this to satisfy the fantasy of doing it with a girl. I had to reassure him... He then again gave me a categorical no. So I was completely depressed that night. My memories are a bit hazy, but in any case, your suggestion in my drunk guy's brain clicked. Then you reminded me of our promise from ten years ago, and I thought to myself that maybe it was a gift of life to be grabbed. This is the moment you threw up on both of us."

Another contraction seized me. I hung onto the seat: it hurt like hell. Opening my eyes again, I realized that we had almost arrived:

"Take the first left, it's there."

The reception was empty, it started well. I walked straight to the maternity ward where I had had all my previous appointments. I forced myself to breathe as I had been taught while waiting for the next contraction. It was nothing like the scenario I had imagined... Emmanuel was not there. John shouldn't have been. And I didn't even know whose the kid was after all.

I prayed with all my being that it was Emmanuel's. It couldn't, or rather it shouldn't be John's. Was there still a chance that my husband would never find out? I couldn't hide it from him. Living with such a secret would be too heavy and above all, it would end up showing. But I had no idea how he would react.

I rushed into the lift.

"So now tell me what got into you..."

"You mean what got into us! We both took a shower to get rid of the vomit. That's where you must have had this memory of me naked with... You know..."

"I guess it wasn't me who put you in this state."

"Well actually... I closed my eyes, I imagined I was with Paul and..."

The lift doors opened. A secretary was behind the reception desk. I grabbed the wood of the counter to secure myself as another contraction assaulted me. The nurse behind the desk observed me, not the least bit surprised. I wasn't the first to arrive in this state apparently.

"Are you OK madam?" she said.

I waited for the pain to pass before I could speak:

"My waters just broke, where should I go?"

"We'll put you in the delivery preparation room. What is your name?"

"Fletcher...Tellier."

Nothing to do, I still had a hard time remembering that I had taken the last name of Emmanuel. She typed it into the computer.

"Can you walk?"

"Yes."

"Okay, so you're going to go to room 103. The midwife is coming in five minutes. You can undress and put on this tunic on so that we can examine you."

She handed it to me, then she pointed to John:

"Is that your husband?"

"No, but he may be the father of the child. My husband is on his way."

The nurse arched an eyebrow and asked in surprise:

"Aren't you sure?"

"Let's say it's complicated. If we do a paternity test, how long does it take to get the results?"

"It depends, generally twenty-four hours, no more."

"And can we do it on a newborn?"

"Yes, after he has passed all the tests, we can take a small blood sample. The father must agree to do one too in order to be able to compare the DNA."

The nurse turned, thinking she was done with us. I objected to her:

"Excuse me, I have one last question. Can my friend come with me until my husband arrives?"

"Yes, of course."

John took me aside.

"Julia, I don't necessarily want to know what's going to

happen in there. I am already not a lover of the feminine gender, but if you want to disgust me forever, this is the best way."

"It didn't seem to turn you off the night we got drunk. Besides, you'll get what's coming to you. You better tell me the rest!"

I didn't feel the next contraction coming. I latched onto the counter again. The secretary approached:

"Take a deep breath Mrs Tellier!"

I breathed, but the pain was so strong. Then it finally subsided.

"I think you'd better get to the delivery preparation room as soon as possible."

John gave me his arm. The midwife arrived as I was trying to put the tunic on, realizing that everyone could see my buttocks when it was on.

"John don't turn round."

I walked over to the observation table, hugging the two sides of the tunic behind me. It wasn't much use since, given the size of my stomach, it didn't close. The midwife came towards me:

"Lie down, please", she said, helping me to do so.

At least that way, John wouldn't see my butt...

"At what time did your water break?"

"About twenty minutes ago."

"How many contractions have you had since?"

"Three, I believe."

"Did you have any other pain? Bleeding?"

"No, nothing abnormal other than that."

"Ok, I'm going to put electrodes on you to monitor the baby's heart rate and your contractions. Beware, it's a bit cold."

She took the electrodes and placed them directly on either side of my stomach. Then she auscultated me and commented:

"The dilation has started. You are at three centimetres.

There should be no complications. Did you ask for an epidural?"

"No, I'm afraid of needles."

"The nurse will drop by to give you a perfusion right now in case there are any complications. I'll send her to you right away. I'll be back every quarter of an hour. If there is an emergency, press that button."

"Would you have a blanket by any chance?"

I didn't want John to see me with my legs in the air.

"Yes, let me give that to you", she answered.

The midwife covered me. She headed for the exit. Suddenly, the anguish that Emmanuel would not arrive in time gripped me and I shouted to her:

"Madam, please wait!"

The midwife retraced her steps.

"How long do you think it's going to take?" I asked her.

"I can't tell you. In general, there is one centimetre of dilation per hour. But that's an average. Every woman is different. You are already three centimetres away. And the cervix must be dilated to ten or twelve centimetres. You still have five to seven hours if you're average. If you're already six centimetres away when I get back, then it'll take a lot less time."

"I'm asking you this because my husband still has an hour and a half or even two hours before he arrives."

She pointed to John:

"This man is not the father?"

"Yes, maybe. Let's say it's a bit complicated..."

"Ok... It can be tight. It's your first one so it should take a little longer than that, but I can't guarantee that. The child may bet here before her father arrives. You will mainly focus on your baby. It doesn't matter who the father is at the moment, the only thing that matters is that you are relaxed for the birth. Take a deep breath with me."

She took my hand. She breathed in and I inhaled, she

breathed out and I did the same.

"There you go, continue like this, relax. Think about your baby."

"Do you think they could both attend the birth?"

"Let's say we could make an exception. But are you sure you want to?"

"If John is the father, I can't deprive him of the birth of his child. So it takes twenty-four hours to find out who the father really is, doesn't it?"

"Yes."

"So it will surely be the longest twenty-four hours of my life..."

"But no, she said. You'll see: the arrival of your child will change everything. It will be really quick."

"If so, we'll see from birth from whose she is."

She left. I pulled up the blanket. The contractions continued to assault me every three minutes.

"John, it's all good, you can turn around, I'm presentable."

He approached me.

"I negotiated so that you could be there for the delivery."

"So I heard, but I'm not sure I want to attend..."

"Whether it's your child or not, this will be your only chance to see this in your life. And then you've already seen me naked once, so that shouldn't shock you... Did Emmanuel call?"

"No, but if you want I can try and reach him."

"I don't know how to break the news to him. To be honest, since I don't remember it, I would rather you tell him. But I'm afraid he'll have a stroke while driving."

"Better not to do this over the phone. It's my fault, I should have told you all about this a long time ago, but I didn't know how."

"John, I am your best friend and I realize that you hid two huge things from me! Did you really think you could keep it a secret all your life?"

"I don't know: I think I was overwhelmed by events. At first I was ashamed to have cheated on Matthias, moreover with a woman. I was afraid of the consequences. And above all, you got together so quickly with Emmanuel... How could I have foreseen that it would be love at first sight between the two of you? Besides, I didn't think for a second that you would get pregnant the first time. Can you imagine the chances of that happening?"

"Well if it's yours, you'll have hit the jackpot! First time you sleep with a chick and bam, you get her pregnant. But hey, you still made love to me, telling yourself that it was the chance of your life. And without a condom..."

"Julia, you were the one who insisted that we don't use one! You told me you wanted a child at any price!"

"Did I say that? But when you saw that I didn't remember anything, you didn't say much either. Do you realize the tsunami it's going to cause in my life if it's yours? How do you think Emmanuel will welcome the news? For all I know I could end up raising this kid on my own..."

"But no, I will never let you down. If it's mine, we'll raise her together. And then Emmanuel will not be able to blame you. You don't remember anything. It's my fault."

"But maybe he'll think I made up the amnesia."

"Julia, Emmanuel loves you more than anything in the world. You are the woman of his life. He just thanks me every day at work for introducing you to each other, so that's not going to change your relationship."

"But what do you know about it? He is waiting for this child like a Messiah! At least as much as me! How will he be able to recover from the fact that I carried the child of someone other than him?"

"Joseph did forgive the Holy Spirit for giving birth to

Jesus."

"Yeah, you are not really the Holy Spirit and I'm even less like the Blessed Virgin..."

"What I mean is that Emmanuel is a Catholic, even if he no longer practices. If he loves you, he will forgive you. And then, this is my crap. I will never let that separate you. Anyway, it might be, that she's his baby. So let's stop freaking out and focus on her."

I nodded.

"I'm going to call Emmanuel to find out where he is without telling him anything and we'll see when he arrives for the rest. You relax like the midwife said and focus on the baby's arrival. See you soon."

John opened the door as the nurse arrived. He let her pass and then left.

"Hello Madam!", she said. "I will put the IV on you. Extend your right arm, please."

I handed it to him and closed my eyes so as not to feel the sting. I breathed, trying to think of something else, but I definitely hated needles the most, and it was unpleasant to feel that I had one stuck in my arm all the time.

"There you go", she said, "I'll come back a little later."

She headed for the exit and John came back to me a minute later.

"So where is he?" I asked impatiently.

"He's about an hour from Paris. There isn't too much traffic according to him. He told me to tell you to wait for him: he's doing as quickly as possible."

"Like it was easy... That gives you an hour to tell me the rest."

Another contraction seized me. John took my hand, but he must have regretted it, as I squeezed it as hard as a stress ball. He withdrew it quickly once the contraction had passed.

"Is that your way of getting revenge on me?"

"Oh, I'm sorry, I didn't realize. So we'd got to the

moment you were soaping me."

"Are you sure you want to talk about it now?"

"Look, I'm to give birth to a baby and I don't know who her father is. If she's yours, I'd at least like to know how she was conceived."

"When we were in the shower, so I started... to have a hard-on", he said quietly, leaning into my ear. "But I saw you noticed it. So I immediately put cold water on it and on you too: I thought it would sober you up, but in fact it didn't really work. We went out, I dried us off and you asked me if you could brush your teeth. Since you were not really able to walk, I carried you to your room. I laid you on the bed, but you stopped me from leaving by putting your arms around my neck. Then you started to kiss me. I didn't think about it, I let it go. You literally jumped on me anyway."

"I can't believe you."

"I assure you, you were insatiable. It's like you've been waiting for this moment for years. Besides you kept saying: 'I've always dreamt of that moment'.

I must have turned all red... But a very violent contraction occurred and I squeezed the hand of John who was not expecting me to twist it again.

"Are you OK?" he said.

"I've been better."

The midwife entered. She looked at the monitor:

"I have the impression that the rhythm of your contractions has become much closer. I need to examine you."

The midwife lifted the blanket.

"You are six centimetres dilated. It's going faster than expected. I think we'll have to take you to the delivery room soon. I'll be back in a quarter of an hour. Sir, if you could get her things together in the meantime."

John nodded.

"Continue to breathe deeply, I'll be right back."

I took a deep breath and then I turned to John. I finally wanted to know what it was really like:

"How long did it last?"

"Erm... I didn't time it."

"And how was it for you?"

"Let's say I wanted to understand how Paul managed to make love to a girl and get her pregnant. Now I know how."

"And how?"

"Closing my eyes and imagining the girl is a man, it's not that bad... But I still prefer men."

"So you're telling me you made love to me thinking about Paul?"

He looked at his feet and whispered barely audibly.

"Yes."

Another contraction arrived. Pain a thousand times worse than a first day of menstruation pierced my stomach. The contractions were getting closer and closer. I didn't even dare to imagine what it would be like when the child came out. I was trying to concentrate on that bloody drunken night! And to think that I still did not remember this historic moment! How was it possible that my memory had not come back?

I screamed again. Damn contractions! I needed the epidural. Too bad about my fear of needles. I was in too much pain. I pressed the button to call the nurse and took the opportunity to continue questioning John while I waited:

"Are you sure what you are saying? Aren't you making the worst joke of my life?"

"No, I promise. This is what I remember. But again, I was drunk too. You fell asleep like a log just after and I went up to Matthias. In the meantime I had taken a shower again so he wouldn't smell you on me. The next day, I wanted to talk to you about it, but I didn't want Matthias to hear us. That's why when you told me you didn't remember anything, I suggested explaining it to you over coffee the next day. Afterwards, I thought about it and I said to myself that if you didn't remember it, it was better not to tell you anything. Especially since Emmanuel was all over you after you left. Matthias had not noticed anything and above all, I saw how much you were under the spell of Emmanuel and I kept everything to myself. Not a day went by that I didn't tell myself it would have been better for me to confess everything. But it took until today for me to find the courage to do so."

Better late than never, I told myself... Again a contraction. I was screaming in pain. They just got bigger. And Emmanuel still wasn't here... I was in so much pain and needed his support right now. And at the same time, I was afraid that he would come. What would be his reaction to the truth? The midwife entered and looked at the monitoring.

"You are practically at one contraction per minute, we will have to take you to the delivery room. Sir, can you please take her things and follow us?"

John obeyed.

"I changed my mind, it hurts too much, I need the epidural."

"Madam, it's too late, you had to have asked for it before reaching 2 inches. Now, it's going too fast, by the time it takes effect you will have already given birth."

"I don't care, I am in too much pain, I beg you!"

I didn't recognize myself. I almost yelled at the poor midwife.

"Madam, listen to me, your child will be arriving in the next hour and I will help you breathe during each contraction to make the pain more bearable. Trust me, I have given birth to thousands. Everything is going to be fine. Okay?"

A contraction again:
"Ahhhhhhhhhhh !!!"

The midwife put her forehead against mine. Then she put my arms around her neck:

"Breathe in with me. Now breathe out."

She did this until the contraction was over. I don't know whether it was because it was calming my panic or because feeling her breathing along soothed me, but the pain was more bearable that way. I wanted to keep her in my arms, but she pulled away. When I think I didn't even know her! Decidedly I was no longer in control of anything.

The midwife disconnected my electrodes, then grabbed the handles of the bed where I was, and asked me to take the stand of the drip in my hand:

"Let's go."

John took the bag, opened the door for the midwife, then followed us. If I had been told eight and a half months ago that it would be my best friend instead of my husband who would attend the birth, I would not have believed it ... In the new ward the nurse who had put in the IV was already there. The midwife positioned me at the centre, then reconnected the electrodes of the device to my belly.

The contractions were coming closer and closer. I screamed in pain each time, but the midwife hugged me and helped me breathe. John came and sat down next to me. She showed him how to do the same thing with me so that he could take over as she watched the baby's head. The midwife removed the blanket.

I was preparing myself psychologically for my vagina to become the object of all the attention. It is unfair that we women have to endure such shame. The guys spend their time ogling other men's cocks in the bathroom and we spend our time hiding our sex as much as possible until that fateful day when it is exposed to everyone. Yet it was far from being as artistic a vision as that of Courbet's *The Origin of the World*. No, it was going to be the butcher's shop. I wasn't even sure I wanted John to see this despite what I had told him earlier.

Suddenly, the memory of seeing a birthing video in biology class when I was a teenager came back to me. It had completely traumatized me: shit was coming out just before the child's head... And when we thought it was the end, there was more to come: the video only stopped when the placenta had been expelled in a pool of blood. I remember a student going out to throw up. As for me, I was not far from it.

The boys cried out in disgust. I realized the unbelievable injustice of being a woman having to carry a child for nine months and then having to bring it out through a mouse hole. But what did I have in mind when I thought about being pregnant? I only saw the result: the cute little being that would come out. I had completely forgotten this documentary until today. All of a sudden, I wasn't so sure I wanted to give birth anymore. John must have sensed my fears. He kissed me on the forehead, took my shoulders in his hands, and looked into mine.

"Don't worry, everything will be all right. Even if Emmanuel doesn't arrive on time, you can count on me."

"But I can't give birth without him! I need him."

As if my baby heard my thoughts, she gave me a kick, as if to say she didn't agree and wanted to get out of here ASAP. A contraction ensued. It hurt like hell and I screamed in pain. John looked at me in panic. He had never seen me like this before. I wasn't sure I wanted him to see the figure of the uncontrollable, rampaging animal that I was becoming in the face of pain.

"We are at nine centimetres", said the midwife. "It won't be long!"

I was panicking.

"John I beg you, go and call Emmanuel to find out where he is."

He left with his mobile. I was angry with my body for

rushing this delivery even though for all my friends it had taken ages. It was all John's fault. No doubt it was a reaction to his revelations. It was as if my body wanted to get it over with as soon as possible so that it could finally know who the father was.

With Emmanuel, at the beginning, we didn't want to know the sex of the baby because I dreamt of a little boy who would look like him. I didn't really want a little girl who would be my spitting image. But Emmanuel had made me give in. He was too curious.

Now I wondered what our child might look like if John was the father. He was straight-haired blond with dark blue eyes and Emmanuel brown with curly hair and brown eyes. As for me, I had been as blonde as wheat when I was little and now I had turned chestnut. Physically speaking, it would be quite complicated to know who the father was, in fact. What would the mixture of our features give? I preferred not to think about it. I was trying to convince myself that it could only be Emmanuel's daughter. But deep down inside, I knew the height of my ovulation period had been on Saturday rather than Monday. All this time I had been expecting John's child. It seemed obvious to me now.

An even more violent contraction broke out. The midwife looked at me:

"If you feel like you have the urge to poo, now is the time to push."

How glamorous was that?! Not something you heard in the movies.

"I can't start without my husband…"

At that moment, John entered the room smiling.

"He should be there in five minutes."

John stood in front of my gaping legs. He looked surprised before quickly looking away when he saw that I was watching him, too. I didn't know what that part of my body looked like now, but I preferred not to imagine it.

Another hyper-violent contraction happened, I screamed again.

"I think it's the moment", said the midwife.

"Can't we wait for my husband to be here, another five minutes?"

"Madam nature does not wait! So you're going to take a deep breath and push really hard. Sir, can you help her up? You are ready? At three. One, two, three, push!"

I did as I had been taught in preparation for childbirth. I must have looked magnificent. I prayed that Emmanuel would arrive as quickly as possible. Please let him run, fly to me! The contractions continued as I pushed under the orders of the midwife. It exhausted me completely. I was sweating. I lay down for a moment, focusing all my thoughts on Emmanuel, as if that could make him arrive.

"The head is engaged, you mustn't stop! Push Mrs Tellier. At three. One, two, three!"

I pushed all I could and felt my child go down more and more. The pain was excruciating and I screamed without any more shame or any regard for the ears of those present. It was stronger than me. I wished I had been put to sleep to stop having to put in all this effort. I was bathed in sweat.

Emmanuel finally pushed the door open. John immediately stepped aside to make room for him to let him kiss me:

"Hello you!"

"I thought you would never arrive."

"I came as fast as I could"

The midwife continued:

"Okay, now that your husband has arrived, I want you to give it your all. Sir, if you could help her up. On the count of three. Inhale. One, two, three, push!"

I pushed like crazy then fell exhausted. Emmanuel stroked my sweaty forehead.

"We see the head, go ahead Madam, push!"

"I can't stand it anymore. It is too hard!"

I stretched out on the bed in unspeakable pain and saw John out of the corner of my eye watching me.

"Madam, breathe in with me... Now breathe out. You'll have to get the head out, once you've done that, the hard part will be over. So you concentrate and at three you push to the maximum. One, two, three, push!"

I felt like my guts were being pierced, but the head was out. I rested in Emmanuel's arms, unable to bear any more pain, with a mad desire to bring this child out of me and not to feel anything like it anymore.

"Come on Mrs Tellier, we must get the shoulders out now. The hardest part is over. Let's go. One, two, three, push!"

I pushed again, screaming and fell back powerless. Emmanuel encouraged me.

"Go on my princess, you're almost there..."

It was sweet, but the remark annoyed me: I looked like anything but a princess right now.

"Come on Mrs Tellier, we must get the other shoulder out. On the count of three! One, two, three, push!"

I felt that the rest of the second shoulder pass. Nothing had prepared me for this. I had no more strength and the midwife kept going...

"Come on, don't relax, keep going, we're almost there. Inhale! One, two, three, push!"

I felt that the rest of the birth lasted for hours. John told me afterwards that it had only taken twenty minutes altogether. But the presence of Emmanuel had given me the strength to continue despite the pain.

I had read that women secrete a hormone during birth that prevented them from hating their child for inflicting the greatest pain of their life...

"It's a girl!" announced the midwife.

Hormones or not, when I received my daughter still covered with the white vernix with which babies are covered at birth and I felt her skin to skin against me, I was overcome with such a feeling of love, that I forgot instantly about how much that little one had hurt me in arriving.

Nature is really well designed. We all looked at each other, completely dazzled by this baby who began instinctivelytto climb up to my breast to suckle it. I devoured this adorable little girl with my eyes. This moment seemed to last forever. Then I caught John's gaze, moved to tears to see this little being who was probably his child–with the vernix, you couldn't really tell... I motioned for him to come closer.

Emmanuel, who had his hand on our daughter's back, looked at me strangely: he had forgotten that John was there. I knew it was time for the truth to come out, but how should I put it? It was for John to do it, not for me. Maybe there would be nothing to add after the baby was washed...

John approached. Emmanuel stepped aside a little to leave room for him and John caressed the baby's head, but she continued to suck. Emmanuel certainly did not understand why John had started to cry silently. Perhaps he interpreted it as an expression of a realization: that he would never have children and that he would witness this miracle for the first and last time.

A nurse stepped forward:

"Mrs Tellier, I'm going to have to take your daughter away from you for a few minutes to give her the necessary tests."

CHAPTER 10
THE TRUTH BENEATH THE VERNIX

I wanted to keep my daughter close to me forever: I didn't want to tear her away from feeding. Above all, I had no desire to find out the truth under the vernix. My instinct was already telling me that John was the father and I didn't want Emmanuel to find out when he saw her after she was washed. Still, living with this secret any longer was intolerable.

"Emmanuel, John is going to tell you something that could potentially turn our lives upside down. But I want you to know that I love you no matter what, just like I will always love this child."

Emmanuel kissed me.

"What do you mean, why do you look so serious?"

"I have only known this myself for a few hours. I'll let you both talk about it."

Emmanuel looked at us, with a questioning air in the face of our dark expression despite the beautiful spectacle of the birth. John made a sign to Emmanuel to follow him. The midwife stopped them with a gesture:

"Not so fast Gentlemen, I need the father to cut the cord."

They both stepped forward. Emmanuel looked askance at John, who gave way. The midwife handed a pair of scissors to Emmanuel, who cut the cord. Then they both left as I hugged my daughter on my breast. I scrutinized her intensely to find out whose she might be.

She was born without hair, which didn't mean much to

me. But the more I looked at her, the more I found that she looked like me. I couldn't quite make out the features of her father in her and the vernix wasn't helping.

The nurse moved closer to my bed to take my baby. Instinct made me hug her harder: I didn't want my child to be torn from me. She seemed to feel so good against me.

"Don't worry, it will only last a quarter of an hour."

Seeing me still attached to my daughter who went on suckling, she added:

"In the meantime, you have to expel the placenta."

I had completely forgotten about that one! Her words had the opposite effect on me. I had no desire to start pushing again, especially without the help of Emmanuel or John. She insisted:

"Ma'am, we really need to check everything now. If we wait too long, your child may undergo lifelong consequences of something that we would not have detected right away after the birth."

She took my daughter in her arms. I felt heartbreak at being separated from my baby. She must have felt the same because she suddenly began to scream.

I suddenly felt a great void when I saw her go away. I wondered what Emmanuel and John could be saying to each other at this very moment. But I didn't have time to dwell on it any longer. The midwife was determined to make me expel this last vestige of my pregnancy.

I was pushing when I saw Emmanuel storming into the bedroom and John with his hand on his cheek following him.

"How could you do that to me?" he yelled.

"Look, until two hours ago, I didn't even have a hint of suspicion about your paternity."

"But how could you forget such a thing?"

"Have you never been so drunk that you can't remember what happened?"

"No", he said visibly exasperated. "And since then, it

still hasn't come back to you? "

"The only thing I remember clearly is from the day before..."

The nurse looked at us dumbfounded:

"Sir! I would like to point out to you that this lady is still in the process of expelling the placenta and that this is not the time for explanations! Instead, please make yourself useful and help her push!"

Emmanuel stood behind me sheepishly. I was pissing blood. I knew his reaction would hurt me, but not that much. I was trying to focus on pushing. The midwife wanted to be sure that no piece of the placenta was left inside. There was a risk of sepsis. Suddenly, she pressed me on the stomach to be sure that there was nothing inside left.

It hurt like hell. I started to cry, feeling all the effects of physical fatigue, pain, but also this gruesome situation. Seeing me in this state, Emmanuel must have felt sorry for me. He stroked my forehead:

"You're going to be all right."

The midwife continued to press on my stomach and I began to sob even more.

"Is it going to be over soon?" I asked desperately.

"I'm sorry ma'am, the nurse replied. I need to be sure that there is nothing left and I can still see pieces."

No one tells you how painful and exhausting giving birth is. Surely this is so you are not discouraged from having children. I wanted to be left alone. I found the courage to look at Emmanuel through my tears as the midwife made me push one last time. He was as pale as death. I had never seen him like this. I closed my eyes for a moment.

"Here Madam, it's over."

"Where's my daughter?"

"She will be back soon, she's being examined. We'll take you to your room and bring her to you right after. I am going to give you sanitary underpants that you will need to change regularly until you are no longer bleeding. You may also have new contractions which will be quite painful. They're here to get everything back in place inside, but they should stop in a few hours. Here, my work is finished. I will come and see you later in your room. The nurse will take you."

The midwife disconnected the electrodes from my stomach and helped me put on the sanitary underpants. I really felt at my most chic. God, a man has to love you to put up with something so gory! And I didn't even know if it was still the case with Emmanuel...

I felt like I had lost him forever. This observation made my tears redouble and I could no longer stop. I was covered and asked to hold the IV pole. Then the bed began to move. When the door opened, I saw John who was waiting outside with red eyes holding a bag of ice to his cheek. He gave me a half smile.

"How do you feel?"

"As if a tank had run over me."

He looked above me in the direction of Emmanuel who was accompanying the nurse. He did not follow us. I still had no idea what they had said to each other and my heart began to beat faster. At that moment, I would have liked to hide at the bottom of a hole.

The nurse positioned the bed in the middle of the room which fortunately was private. She made sure the drip was working and showed me the emergency button. She told me she would be back with the baby in a few minutes. Emmanuel waited for her to go. Then he took a chair and sat down next to me.

"I would understand that it's impossible to forgive me", I told him. "That you now want to leave me."

"I don't know Julia, I need time."

I told him how desperate I had been, just before I met him, to find a man who would have children with me and

I tried to justify that crazy idea. I told him how I had probed Matthias and then abandoned the project. Then I told him the few details I still remembered after this famous drunkenness.

He was silent for a moment. I couldn't hold back my tears from falling. Suddenly, I was convinced that he had ceased to love me.

The nurse came back with my daughter.

"Do you want me to put her in your arms or in her bed?"

"Give her to her father, please."

Emmanuel looked at me puzzled. He took her against him and the magic of babies operated: in her presence, he softened. It was impossible to resist her.

"She looks just like you", he said.

The nurse leaned over to stroke her cheek:

"In any case, she is in perfect health: we have done all the tests and everything is fine. Do you want to breastfeed her?"

"Yes, she already started just after she was born..."

"Were you shown how to position her?"

She propped the pillows under me while helping me sit up, then addressed Emmanuel:

"Sir, can I borrow her?"

"Of course", he said and gave the baby away.

But when she separated from Emmanuel, Clara began to cry. The nurse told me:

"Open your tunic."

I opened it and she put my screaming daughter against me. She was at the height of my breast and she began to suck instinctively.

"There she was, hungry as hell!" the nurse exclaimed. You keep her that way, and if the position becomes uncomfortable, feel free to switch breasts or readjust. I'll be back in a quarter of an hour so we can change her nappy and dress her together.

She left the room. I caught Emmanuel's tender gaze on us, but his smile died away as soon as he noticed that I was watching him.

"If this is my daughter, I think I would still blame John for stealing what was to be the happiest day of my life. I look at you both and I keep wondering if she is really my child."

"There is only one way to find out. I asked the midwife before delivery how long it takes to get the results of the paternity test: they can be obtained in twenty-four hours."

I didn't know how to convince him of my amnesia. I ventured:

"I ask you not to blame us. It happened before I even knew you. All along, I was convinced that this child was yours. But only this test will prove it. Whatever the outcome, I have not stopped loving you and I would still like to bear you another child. You are the man of my life. I do not want to lose you."

"Me neither, but I don't know if I could bear to see a child growing up before my eyes who is not mine."

Someone knocked on the door and then entered. It was the midwife:

"Well, I see she still has a good appetite. How do you feel ?"

"I've felt better."

"I think you need to be changed."

"I'm not sure I can move with the little one."

"Don't worry, I'll help."

"Wait, can my husband avoid having to witness this?"

Emmanuel turned to face the wall. She lifted the blanket and changed my bloody underpants. I felt at my most glamorous…

"We took a sample of your baby's blood and we're going to analyze it, but these gentlemen should go and do it right away as well."

Emmanuel followed her. I was alone with my

daughter... My baby almost made me forget that she had just cast a shadow over our common future by telling me that he could not stand it if she was John's child.

We had agreed names with Emmanuel for a boy or a girl, but I dared not call her Clara. After all, if John was the father, he too was name her.

In all this turmoil, I only wanted one thing: that she would be happy and that she would not be affected by the irresponsibility of her mother during a crazy night too drenched in calva that she did not even remember.

My daughter had fallen asleep on my breast, happy and sated. She had no idea for a single second that her two potential fathers were fighting each other with blood tests to declare their rule over her.

The nurse returned. I motioned to her not to make too much noise so as not to wake my daughter. So she began to whisper:

"We are going to put her in bed and test your urination."

Here was yet another thing! What the hell was that?

"My urination?"

"Yes, we need to check that your urogenital system is working properly after giving birth: you will have to urinate."

I cried out:

"In front of you?"

"No, not in front of me. I'll help you go to the bathroom and you'll tell me if you can or not."

What a joy to be a mother!

"Are you sure it's not going to wake her up if we put her to bed?"

"No. She also went through a hell of an ordeal earlier. She's tired, trust me."

"I'm not sure that I'll be able to move around."

Just getting up hurt too much.

"Don't worry, you still have a few more hours like this,

but it will get better. Here, I am going to take your baby and put her in bed and then I will help you out of yours."

She took my daughter gently and put her in her cot on wheels, which she then pushed aside so that she could get closer to my bed.

"Please don't hesitate to lean on me. I will hold you."

I felt like a grandmother in a nursing home, unable to pee without someone accompanying her. The nurse helped me sit on the toilet bowl.

"I'll be waiting for you at the door."

"It would help me to drink a bit of water", I told her because I hadn't drunk anything since I left the apartment.

"Let me give you that."

She took a plastic cup from the sink and filled it with water, then handed it to me.

I drank it as she went out of the bathroom. She had left the door ajar so that she could hear me. I took off my bloodstained underpants and tried to pee. My "urogenital equipment" felt a bit pressured especially after my daughter's bulldozer had run over it. I managed to squeeze out a few drops. It was definitely very embarrassing and humiliating. Now I had to tell an unknown nurse that I had managed to pee.

"A few drops, does that count?"

"Yes."

I got rid of my used underpants by throwing them right in the middle of the bin under the sink. Hole in one! I tried to put on a new one from the ones available next to it.

"Would you like some help?"

I was ashamed to say yes, but I had no strength left and it was a pain to get up from the toilet on my own to put it on.

"Yes, please."

She came back to help me then put me back in my bed. My daughter took the opportunity to wake up.

"Perfect, we'll be able to change and dress her, I'll let

you watch how I do and then I'll help you lie down. You too need rest."

My dazed daughter was whimpering as she was changed. She groaned slightly as the nurse put her back in bed and fell asleep again almost immediately. The nurse helped me to lie down and closed the curtains. She pulled the door open on her and I fell asleep almost immediately as deeply as my daughter... I had never been so tired in my life.

*
* *

I woke up alerted by my baby's cries, I don't know how long after I fell asleep, but it didn't seem very long to me given how tired I felt... I opened one eye and sat up as best I could. John was holding my baby in his arms and was trying to calm her down. Emmanuel was there and held her hand, doing nice little smiles. I wondered if I was not dreaming. I looked at them both questioningly. John spoke:

"Emmanuel and I decided on a truce until the results and to take advantage of Clara together."

I thought it was a joke. This seemed much too adult and reasonable a decision to be true.

"Are you sure?" I answered. "I mean... you slapped John earlier, and now it's a truce?"

"Yes", said Emmanuel.

"We don't see why our little one should be separated from her father or her future godfather, says John. And then she's too cute for us to go to war today. We will see tomorrow."

I couldn't believe my ears. What happened during my sleep? John handed me my daughter.

"I think our little Clara would like to return to her mother's arms to eat."

"What did you call her?"

"Clara. Isn't it the name you chose for her? I think it's suits her perfectly."

Emmanuel helped me get up on the pillows, then John put Clara in my arms. I opened my tunic so that she could suck. She did not need to be asked twice: this child was voracious...

"Hello my little Clara", I said to her.

The two boys looked at her with infinite tenderness and I watched them incredulously.

"But what are we going to do if John is the father?"

"The truce also applies to you Julia... We will talk about it only when we know, that is to say tomorrow around 3pm. In the meantime, the three of us will take care of Clara and celebrate her coming into this world. When the results arrive, we will decide."

We spent the day together without telling the outside world of our daughter's arrival. She took her first bath surrounded by the three of us. We were all completely overjoyed with her. I realized that it was she who had managed to bring my man and my best friend to their senses, just by being a little enchanting baby. John left us in the evening.

The havoc that his silence had caused had surely made John decide not to hide anything more and to go face Matthias to tell him this part of the story. I had left my keys with John so that he could sleep at our home in case it turned into a fight. Anyway, Emmanuel was going to stay and sleep at the hospital with me. He was not yet aware that his brother Paul was having sex with John and I certainly wasn't going to tell him about it.

What was certain was that if John was the father, it was going to be quite a mess for our daughter: she was going to have a hard time understanding that her mother was dating the brother of her father's childhood love... If you managed to understand this sentence, bravo!

For now, I preferred not to think about it. I focused on my daughter and tried to recoup the few hours of sleep my body was asking for. Which was not really easy because Clara asked to suckle every two hours.

Fortunately, Emmanuel did everything to make my job easier and bring her to me so that I didn't have to get up. Which I couldn't do anyway given the pain that assailed me even when I sat up. On the other hand–and this made me very sad–Emmanuel was helping me, but he was cold. He didn't kiss me, didn't hug me. I discovered a distant man whom I didn't know.

John arrived quite late the next morning after having slept at our place. He had confessed everything to Matthias, even about Clara. He had reacted rather quite badly and had told him to leave without letting him take his things.

John hoped that Matthias would come to his senses in a while and that they could talk about the separation of their properties. But for the moment, John understood that he did not want to hear from a guy who had always loved another in secret, and who in addition cheated on him with his best girlfriend, who had perhaps given birth to their. child.

I was sad for Matthias whom I had always liked. I definitely couldn't look myself in the mirror since I knew the end of this story...

Time passed very quickly until the fateful hour. The nurse arrived with the results around 3:15 p.m. Clara was in my arms and the three of us were very tense.

"Ladies and Gentlemen, here are the results."

She handed an envelope to Emmanuel. He opened it, then suddenly crumpled I took the letter too and turned pale. Then I handed it to John, who also turned white as a sheet. I could not believe it:

"Are you sure?"

"Perfectly sure", answered the nurse.

How could I doubt it? It was marked in black and white. The messenger slipped away, feeling that she was too much in this tense atmosphere. The conundrum was exploding in my head. I exclaimed:

"What are we going to do now?"

Emmanuel was seated, his head in his hands. I suspected what he might be feeling. The woman of his life had carried another's child for almost nine months. John ended up saying:

"It doesn't matter who the biological father is. It's your daughter, it's you the couple. I don't want that to change anything from what was planned. I will be his godfather and I will take the secret to the grave if necessary. I would feel bad my entire life if this fatal night separated you. You are made for each other and you will have other children together anyway."

"But that's not possible", I replied. "She's your daughter too. At some point everyone will see that you are her father."

"Not if she's not told", answered John.

Emmanuel got up:

"I could never keep this a secret to myself. Yesterday must have been the best day of my life and you ruined it for me. How could you do something like that to me, John, when you knew we were going to meet Julia the next day? And you Julia?"

Even if I had to carry the weight of my fault, I was fed up with Emmanuel blaming me for a fact that I had absolutely no recollection of and which had occurred before I even met him...

"But damn it, I didn't even know you when Clara was conceived! You can blame me as much as you want, but it was John who didn't say anything. And then that doesn't change the problem: Clara didn't ask for that. She doesn't give a damn about having a father or two! All she needs is love and security. So I ask you the question again: how are we going to raise this child?"

Emmanuel took his coat and went towards the exit.

"Where are you going?"

"It's your child, it's up to you to decide."

"But you're going to come back?"

"I have no idea."

And he slammed the door. If I could have got up and chased after him, I would have.

"I beg you John catch him up, quickly!"

John began to run after Emmanuel. He came back two minutes later empty-handed while I tried to calm Clara who had started to cry. It was all over. The truth was too hard to swallow...

I couldn't blame him. His reaction was normal. I already saw my future as a single mother all laid out. I started to cry. John got close to me and took me in his arms. Clara was crying with me. He tried to calm us both down.

"I'm sorry. I feel so stupid for not saying anything."

"What is done is done."

I was torn between two contradictory feelings: on the one hand I hated John and on the other I couldn't blame him. What am I saying?... blame us. Finally my stupid plan had succeeded against all odds and had only sown misfortune around it. Only Clara who demanded our full attention brought us back to reality. It was time for her bath and we automatically made the movements that the three of us had done yesterday. I felt like I was dead inside, even though I tried to hold on for my daughter.

"You will have to declare her birth", I said to John. "With your name."

"Are you sure?"

"She might have Emmanuel's last name, but I want her to know that she's your daughter anyway."

"I'm not sure, you know. Let's wait for him to come back."

"There have been enough lies like this. Please declare her and call Emmanuel to ask if he wants to come with you."

"You know, I would like us to give her our three names."

"Why?"

"Because even though I'm the progenitor, she's still your daughter. He's the one who will raise her more than me."

I started to cry even more.

"John, he's just left. I have no idea if he will ever come back. Do what you see fit."

He took me in his arms.

"Leave me alone!" I shouted at him, pushing him away. "I'm sorry, but now I can't take it."

"Are you going to be fine alone with Clara?"

"Do I have a choice?"

I started to cry again. I was a single mother. Everything I had wanted to avoid.

He left after giving Clara a kiss on the forehead. She fell asleep on my breast and I found myself alone and in physical pain and a crushed heart on top of it.

My mobile was on the bedside table. I dialled Emmanuel's number. He didn't answer I didn't want to speak to him by answering machine. So I redialed the phone number. This time, I got the answering machine directly. He didn't want to talk to me... I started to write him a text, but deleted the content. Then I started again. But what could I say?

I ended up sending him the simplest message in the world.

I love you. I need you. I miss you.

I waited a good two hours for him to answer before

John came back. But in vain. All the while, I had cursed myself. Why had life followed through on my plan? I could have had it all, and now I had nothing. If he left me forever, I didn't know how I was going to get over it. How was I going to raise Clara on my own? I wouldn't even have the pleasure of seeing her father's face in her eyes.

John returned with the birth certificate. Clara Langlois-Tellier. She should have been called Clara Fletcher-Tellier.

"They didn't want to take your maiden name into account, now that you're Mrs. Tellier."

"What a bunch of sexists at the town hall! But hey, I must admit that it would have been too long anyway..."

How was I going to explain this to my daughter when the time came? What kind of example was I? John seeing me still so sad, took me in his arms:

"Did he call?"

"No. I tried to reach him several times, but I only reached his answering machine."

"I went to your apartment a while ago after the town hall to see if Emmanuel was there. He took some of his belongings and I think he's gone. But I have an idea... I would like you to follow me in Normandy when you leave the hospital."

"Are you mad?!"

"Listen, I can't go back to my apartment in Paris because of Matthias who hates me. Clean air won't hurt Clara and maybe Emmanuel has taken refuge with his parents. I can use the ten-day paternity leave at the office and work from home until you resume your job. Afterwards I will commute to Paris once a week, rearranging all my appointments. That's what I've always dreamt of doing anyway: living in Normandy."

"Yes, but not me. Not with Emmanuel's parents around."

"They are at the other end of the bay. During all the

weekends that I have spent there with Matthias since we got home, I never saw them."

"But I have a lot of paperwork to do in Paris."

"You can be like me and concentrate everything into one day."

"What about my belongings and the baby's stuff?"

"I have a friend who has a van. I can borrow it and take everything to Le Tréport tomorrow. I can set everything up in my cottage and come back to pick you up when you are released from the hospital. When will you be discharged?"

"Tomorrow late afternoon if all goes according to plan."

"Perfect. It will do you good to be far from Paris and in the countryside. It's called maternity leave, right? It will give Emmanuel time to think. Anyway, I'll see him at work again and try to convince him to come back by any means. Give him time to digest this news. In any case, we will find a solution to raise this child, I promise you."

"You seem very optimistic to me. I don't think Emmanuel is coming back. In my opinion, he will do everything to avoid us. I even wonder if he will not resign from work in order not to have any contact with you."

"And how would he pay for the apartment you bought together? He cannot afford to quit."

"Knowing him, he might do what you plan. Telework and return to Normandy. It's his dream too. I will just have to sell our apartment. Anyway, I couldn't pay for it on my own."

"Listen, we'll see, for the moment let's wait and see how Emmanuel will react. I advise you not to give him any news. It will eventually intrigue him and he will inevitably wonder what has become of you and how you are managing with Clara without him."

"I would still like to leave him a note at home to let him know that we are safe."

"Ok, but don't tell him where you're going. It will force him to get in touch with you to get the information. I'll find you some paper. I'll put your letter on display on the living room table. Anyway, I have to go to organise the move."

"You're crazy. And I'm even crazier to follow you."

"I'm not going to leave my best friend and my daughter in trouble. I told you that I'll always be there for you. And then time heals everything."

"Says the man who fell back into the arms of his youthful love as soon as he saw him again."

"I thought I was cured. If he had never crossed my path again, I would have continued as if nothing had happened."

"But you bought a cottage in his parents' village to meet him again. And that's exactly what happened."

"Ok, I admit... I'll get you some paper."

John helped me write the letter.

> Emmanuel, I can't stay in this apartment knowing you're not here. I am taking Clara far from Paris until the end of my maternity leave. I took her things and mine. You know how to reach me ... I love you and will never stop loving you. I'm waiting for you... Julia.

John left to organize everything. I secretly hoped he would meet Emmanuel the next day so he could convince him to come back. But that didn't happen. No sign of him. At work, John had just heard that Emmanuel had taken a week's leave. He could be anywhere.

CHAPTER 11
BABY BLUES

He had abandoned me... I kept crying all the time. I had read that the days after leaving the hospital could cause baby blues. Also, I had heard that when you had to accept the disappearance of someone who was still alive, it was called white mourning. Poetic expression for an unmanageable situation! How could one forget a person alive but not sending any news? Clara must have felt my pain because she was crying all the time too.

Poor John was trying as best he could to cheer us both up, but being in his cottage in Tréport only reminded me of the day I met Emmanuel and the weekends we spent here making love. I lost myself in the memory of those happy moments that would never come back. Part of me still believed in Emmanuel's return and every time I went for a walk along the coast with Clara, I hoped to see him appear at the other end of the bay, where his parents had their home. But I never saw him.

John took care of everything. He did the shopping, changed Clara, calmed her down when she cried, brought her to me to breastfeed her and tried to make me laugh with stupid jokes. He managed to get a few smiles from me, but the melancholy still took hold of me. I imagined the indescribable happiness that would have been the first days of Clara's life with Emmanuel in our Paris apartment.

I felt I had aged overnight. About ten white hairs had appeared. More pronounced wrinkles too. I couldn't even find the strength to put on makeup or do my hair anymore. Everything cost me. Take a shower or even going out.

My body was slowly recovering from childbirth, but seeing myself naked scared me. My stomach sagged and my breasts full of milk seemed to flow constantly: I finally understood the meaning of the word mammal. I felt like a foster mother, but not like a woman.

I wondered if one day I would regain my body from before. But I already knew the answer: surely never. So I avoided looking at myself naked in the mirror because it depressed me.

We had been at Le Tréport for a week when John received a phone call from Paul. He came the following weekend to see his father who was still recovering from his operation and to help his mother a bit. He wanted to know if John was there for the weekend and if he could drop by after lunch on Saturday.

This news was like a boost to me. I hoped that Paul might be able to tell me more about Emmanuel who was still observing radio silence. Maybe he could convince his brother to come back as he was surely in touch with him.

As for John, he was so happy to see the love of his life again and his joy was infectious. The day before his arrival, he had spent the evening scrubbing the cottage from top to bottom and playing music to which he danced while cleaning. He pretended to sing into the vacuum cleaner tube to impress Clara who looked at him without ceasing to cry, terrified by the noise of the device. But John's joy was contagious and I took Clara in my arms and started dancing to *I feel good* by James Brown while John continued his facial expressions to make us laugh.

The next day, I put on makeup for the first time in a week. I wanted to make a good impression on Paul and I tried not to cry. Instead, I tried to leave room for hope in my heart.

Paul arrived at John's while I was breastfeeding Clara and I let them both hug. It was the first time that I had seen the pair of them together. They had arrived hand in hand, magnificent, surely one of the most beautiful gay couples I had ever seen. The sight of Paul made my heart ache: he looked so much like Emmanuel. He let go of John's hand when he saw me.

"Don't worry Paul, she knows."

"Oh, you told her…"

"Yes, she's my best friend. And the mother of my daughter…"

The question was burning me and I couldn't wait any longer:

"Hi Paul. Did you see Emmanuel?"

"Yes, he's with my parents right now."

"Does he know I'm here?"

"No. I myself didn't know that I would see my niece here…"

He approached Clara who had just finished breastfeeding and was resting quietly in my arms.

"What a beauty! Can I take her?"

I handed her to him. Paul took Clara gently in his arms and observed her. She was almost fourteen days old now and her eyes, not yet their final colour, were beginning to tend towards her father's blue. Her nose looked more like John's than mine, but the rest of her face and her hair was mine.

"She looks just like you", said Paul.

"Yes, I know, but I hope she will inherit John's eyes."

"I think she's off to a good start…"

Then he said:

"You both look exhausted."

"We don't sleep much", I answered. "Clara wakes up every three hours. But luckily John helps me a lot: he managed to have his paternity leave validated, but it will be a little harder afterwards because he will be back to work next week."

"How did they react at work, Paul asked John, when you said you had become a father overnight?"

"They didn't believe me. They know I'm gay. I had to pull out the birth certificate so they could see it was true. But maybe Emmanuel had already told the whole story at work."

"I'm not sure of it. He came directly to my parents after learning that he was not the father. My mum kept telling him that he would have done better to stay with his ex instead of choosing an atheist like you with questionable sexual morals."

That didn't surprise me coming from Marie-Bénédicte. Always true to herself!

"She's brainwashing him all the time", Paul continued. "She tells him that he has to forget you and start his life over with someone else."

I was stunned:

"What?!

"You know my mother. She doesn't want this story to tarnish their reputation at church on Sunday mornings."

"What about Emmanuel, what does he say to that?"

"As far as I can tell, this event has ravaged him. I tried to chat with him last night, but he's silent. I've never seen him like this. He is content to attend meals without touching much of what is on his plate. He listens with one ear to my mother's diatribes against you and with the other, to the whining of our recovering father. The rest of the time, he works away in his room, even on weekends. He hardly goes out. As if work was going to make him forget what had happened."

John tenderly wrapped his arms around Paul and they both looked at Clara. I envied them.

"So he's not feeling any better than me?" I asked.

"No, not really, answered Paul."

"Do you think you could let him know I'm here and ask him to come see me? He hasn't answered any of my calls or texts. I can't take this situation anymore. I know he can't forgive me and feels betrayed, but I need him. I am ready to do anything to make him come back."

"Even to abandon your daughter?"

"What do you mean?"

"The only thing he told me was that he wanted to wake up from this nightmare and get everything back to how it was before Clara was born."

I was dumbfounded. I could never live without my daughter, it would be like ripping out a part of me. But I couldn't even think of giving up on Emmanuel for a second. I really hoped he would never ask me to make such a choice.

"Don't worry, if there is one person who can reason him, it's me. Anyway, I intend to announce something very important tonight at dinner. I think my dad can face it now."

John turned to face Paul.

"Is it true? Did you tell your wife?" asked John.

Paul nodded. John then kissed him with such passion that I began to fear for my daughter who was between them.

"You don't want to pass me Clara?" I asked John, who handed her to me.

I let them carry on while I looked at my daughter. Could I give up the flesh of my flesh for Emmanuel?

"I'm going to leave the two of you", I announced to them. "I'm going out for a walk on the beach with her."

"Don't feel like you have to go."

"You have lots of things to talk about and your life together to organize. I just have one question: How are you going to manage about your children?" I asked Paul.

"Audrey has filed for divorce and at the moment I will have the children every other week. It's not a lot, but it's better than nothing. My children and my wife will certainly never forgive me, but I can no longer live a lie."

I left them. As I was walking on the beach, I wanted to go and meet Emmanuel since he was there. I decided to send him a text.

> Paul just told me that you are with your parents. I'm on the beach, come and join me...

I stood in front of their family home, but did not see him. I didn't dare ring the bell.

Clara was asleep. It was very cold, but the sky was completely clear. I wondered how much longer Emmanuel was going to remain silent and avoid facing the situation. After all, I was his wife. Maybe he sent divorce papers to me at our Paris address? Maybe he didn't love me anymore?

I felt a presence behind me. I turned around, but it was a stranger walking on the beach. My heart wanted to find Emmanuel everywhere.

I hoped that an hour of privacy would have been enough for the boys. I texted John to let him know I was coming back. I wondered how Paul could have made such a difficult decision to abandon his wife and children and go and live with the love of his life. Well, give up... he would continue to see them, but no longer on a daily basis.

What would life be like without Clara? I could only imagine an immense void. Even though she kept me awake, it was a very small sacrifice in the face of the joy she brought me.

I had always wanted to be a mother. I was naturally made for it, but it was more than instinct. This urge, this need to give someone love had always been there. I wanted to do everything to make this child happy after I had burdened her with a father who was not my husband. Even if Emmanuel agreed to live with my daughter and be her stepfather, there would inevitably be a heartbreak. Whether it was me who saw her less or John, one of us would always feel aggrieved. Living under the same roof could only be a short-term solution.

I didn't imagine how I could live with John and Paul on one side and Emmanuel on the other. The question of intimacy would not be easy. And then, what about a second child? How do you explain that his or her sister has two dads and that he or she only has one?

When we returned, John and Paul were sitting in the living room and had prepared tea. I started to undo Clara's coat. She screamed and I tried in vain to calm her down. John took her in his arms and very slowly succeeded in consoling her:

"I think I'm going to change her", he said.

Paul poured me some tea:

"We spoke with John and we made a decision: we would like to live together. "

"Here?"

"Yes. At the moment, I can only be there every other weekend. Unlike John, I cannot telework because my clients are in Dijon. On the other hand, we will be living together on the weekends here first, if you agree."

"You know, I don't feel at home in this cottage and besides John only owns half at the moment..."

"Precisely, things are progressing with Matthias. John offered to buy Matthias's half of the cottage in Le Tréport and then Matthias can buy my half of the Paris apartment. They are due to meet in Paris next week to sort out the details."

"What about you, what are you going to do in Dijon?"

"I'm going to rent an apartment. It will allow me to see the children until I move here permanently."

It was clear that I couldn't stay here with Clara once he was settled here. He continued:

"I will suggest to my father that I work with him as a lawyer. He always wanted me to take over his business: his dream will finally come true. It should allow me to live here full time in three or four months and find another lawyer in Dijon to replace me."

"But you haven't told your parents yet, how do you think they're going to take the shock?"

"I don't know. Either way, they have no choice. I will not go back. I will never again sacrifice my happiness for convenience."

"I'm going to have to go back to work in Paris at the end of March and I still don't know where I'm going to live, since Emmanuel remains walled in his silence."

"Don't worry, tonight I'm going to shake it. I'll tell him he can't leave you like this without talking to you."

"In any case, the question of Clara will arise."

"She can stay with us or go with you, it's as you wish."

"I don't know if I can take care of her by myself."

"But of course you can, you'll see. We will find a solution."

"But I don't want to be separated from her and I don't want to separate her from her father either."

"In that case, you'd have to find work around here."

"But it's impossible. There is nothing around. And then forgive me for telling you that like that, but I absolutely do not dream of living fifteen minutes away on foot from your mother."

He laughed.

"You're wrong, she's her granddaughter, like it or not. And you will surely be glad that she can look after her for you."

"I still prefer to leave her with my mother… And if you came to join me instead?"

"Personally, I hate Paris. Dijon was a compromise that I had made with my wife because her job was there and I could work as a lawyer anywhere in France, but I only dream of one thing: to live here with John again."

"And you are not afraid of what will be said?"

"No, I know everyone in the area. If they are not happy with the turn my life has taken, they are free to stop talking to me. Here, nature is a stone's throw away and I miss the sea air when I stray from it for too long."

"I think your brother is the same. He dreams of coming back to settle here. I would have to speak with John. At the moment, I don't feel ready to live without my daughter even for a few days..."

"You don't have to make a decision right away, you know. We still have a little time. I myself have to break the news to my family already. Besides, I have to go. I said I was going for a walk, but I have to help my mum with dinner tonight."

"Are you coming back for the night?"

"Yes, after dinner."

"Don't worry, I will most certainly be excommunicated by my family, so I'll be back soon. Maybe I can convince Emmanuel to come too."

"Don't give me false hope…"

"I will still try because I can't stand to see him in this state. He needs to understand that this is not your fault, and that it happened before you met him. Besides, I'm a bit angry with you for having made love with the man of my life..."

I blushed, lowering my eyes.

"But considering the result, you did well!" said Paul to reassure me.

"If I still don't remember it, maybe it wasn't that transcendent!"

He laughed as John arrived with the little one...

"That's not what you said that night my dear," John retorted.

"Well, I think we'll end this conversation here before Clara starts blushing," I said.

"Anyway, I have to get on," said Paul before kissing John.

It was new for me to see two men showing affection because when John was in a relationship with Matthias, they never showed any in front of me. They maintained a kind of modesty in public under all circumstances.

I was going to have to get used to it quickly since Paul was going to be living with us on weekends. I couldn't imagine what it must have been like for them to live their love secretly all through their teenage years. Maybe it was just because of this that their feelings were so strong?

Would Paul bear the heartbreak of no longer living with his children? Time would tell... I was trying to imagine if Emmanuel had told me he was gay. It would have been as if I believed I was building a life on solid foundations when in fact it was just a sandcastle. That's exactly what Emmanuel must have been saying to himself right now. I had betrayed his trust, without knowing it and unwittingly, but the consequences remained the same.

Paul had tried to be like everyone else: to live the life his parents had laid out for him, to fight his very nature. I wondered how his sex life was with Audrey. Did he think of John all the time while making love to her? They had had three children after all! I asked John the question when Paul left:

"Tell me, I was thinking... is Paul bi? I mean, how did he manage to have three children with Audrey?"

"Funnily enough, that's one of the first things I asked him when we got together... He told me he thought of me every time."

"Kind of like when you made love to me."

"Yes, I admit it. I've had a few men in my life, but I've never stopped thinking about Paul when I've been with other men."

"But they weren't turning you on?"

"I'd be lying if I told you they weren't. Only, I never found in them the gentleness or the sense of belonging that I had with Paul. He's like my soul mate, you know..."

"And how come you kept this part of your life completely hidden until the day I gave birth? I'm your best friend, yes or no? I thought we were telling each other everything..."

"I'm sorry Julia, I couldn't tell you about it. It would have been like talking about a mirage. I thought I would never be with Paul again. And it hurt too much."

"But you bought a cottage here hoping to see him again..."

"Yes, that was a crazy hope... But I knew he was just as crazy about this area as I was. We had both painted the town red, and I always knew if we had to meet up, it would be there. I was afraid it would come out accidentally in a conversation with Matthias if I told you. And then we all know you don't have a tongue in your pocket when you've been drinking."

"Stop making fun of me! Anyway, I now understand how well you can keep a secret. I mean, eight and a half months without admitting to me that I was potentially pregnant with your child... Are you sure there's nothing left in the cupboard?"

"No, I promise that's it, I don't have anything hidden in the cupboard."

"You'd better not, because next time it's not my waters that will break, I'm going to have a heart attack if you tell me something that big."

"I promise, there is nothing else."

"Uh yes, there is a small detail. According to Paul, you are not coming back to live in Paris: he has just told me that you want to settle here. Which is a bit of a problem for our daughter. I can't imagine being apart from her. And then, I don't even know where I'm going to live now..."

"We're going to wait a bit before making decisions ... I'm sure Emmanuel will be back."

"How can you be so sure? He has not been in touch since the birth! Besides, he knows I'm here, but he still hasn't shown up... The worst part is that Paul suggested that I should give up my daughter to be with him..."

"What do you mean?"

"I don't know. He said something to me like: "Would you be willing to give up your daughter for Emmanuel?" But I'm definitely not ready to give her up."

"He probably meant that at first it would be good if you could be together without the little one."

"While breastfeeding, that seems difficult to me. Besides, I don't see how he's going to get used to the idea that he's her adopted father if he doesn't see her. But I'm talking like he's coming back, when he might never do..."

I burst into tears. It was a habit lately... John hugged me, but it wasn't his touch that I wanted. This made my tears redouble. I was in despair to have lost the man of my life forever and to have ruined everything because of having been intoxicated...

"First, I think you need to find yourself. Maybe without the little one first. Know that I will be there for her no matter what. You gave me the greatest gift in the world, something I never expected... I can't thank you enough! My job is in Paris so I will inevitably go there frequently for one or two days a week or even longer if the traffic is bad. We can arrange for me to pick up Clara when I'm there and bring her back here for the weekend."

"But when she goes to school how will we manage? And then do you think it's okay for a kid to have five hours of back and forth driving a week?"

"At the moment, I don't see any other possible solution. Unless you come and live here too?"

"Are you out of your mind?"

"Alright, ok. Let's say we keep Clara between Paris and Le Tréport. Think about all those parents who complain all the time about having their kids full time. You will have your weekends or your weeks quiet while I keep the little one with Paul."

"And if I want to spend more time with her?"

"There are the holidays... We'll work it out. What I

mean is we will do everything to make it work."

"I find it hard to imagine going a single day without seeing her..."

"I know."

John hugged us both and kissed me on the forehead. When I closed my eyes, I would have thought it was Emmanuel. But those moments I had dreamed of so much before giving birth would probably never exist. Where was I going to live?

"What if I miss her first steps or her first words?" I asked.

"You know, she might well say her first words and take her first steps with the nanny. We can always make videos for each other: it will make memories for her too."

"I have a feeling she will necessarily be deprived of one of us more than the other."

"But no... She will see that both parents are happy and then she will understand later. We'll explain it to her as soon as she asks any questions."

"It might be a hell of a lot of fun when she starts to ask us how she was born. I can already see the explanation: "So your mum was drunk. And of course Clara will say: "What does that mean drunk?". So I will have to explain that what I did was wrong, and that you shouldn't do the same because it can make you lose your memory. Then I'll have to explain to her that her father didn't want to die without having sex with a girl, and besides that he got me pregnant right before I met the man who should have been her father. And then I should explain to her why her "uncle" lives with her daddy."

"I'll admit it's no picnic, but before she's talking and asking that kind of question, we're going to have at least two, three years to prepare."

Paul arrived around 11:00 p.m. Alone. Clara was lying down and John was reading while I dozed tiredly on the couch watching TV.

"So?" John asked Paul while helping him to take off his coat.

"Well", answered Paul, "I waited for dessert to tell them I was gay."

"And how did they react?"

"Let's say it went better than I had hoped: my mother began to sob and then called you names: "All that is the fault of this depraved John Langlois who converted my son to the ways of Satan". When I told them that I was divorcing Audrey my mother was beside herself: "But what are you thinking about? You don't get divorced in the Tellier family!" And when I said that I was going to move here with you in a few months and that I wanted to work with my father in order to take over his law firm, he replied that it was a good idea and that he had always dreamt of it."

"Seriously?" said John, taken aback.

"Yes. And my dad also said he always knew I was gay."

I couldn't stay silent.

"What about Emmanuel?" I asked.

"He said nothing. Oh now that I think of it, when my mother called John all names, he said something like John was the man through whom all misfortunes happened."

"It's screwed", I sighed. "He will never come back."

"I'm not so sure about that", said Paul.

"Why?

"Because when it was time to leave, he held me back to ask me about you."

"Ah. And what did you say to him?"

"How stupid he was to let the woman of his life slip away for something she couldn't even remember. That you love him, that you await his return, and that he owes it to you at least to come out of his silence so that you can plan your future with your daughter, if only to find out if you are still husband and wife. And finally I reminded him that as a Catholic, he had to find the strength to forgive you. That John had only committed the crime of being silent, thinking it was better for everyone, and that he was also convinced that he could in no way be the father of the child."

"Yeah well, you weren't that sure," I remarked to John.

Paul paid no attention to me and went on:

"Either way the damage is done and he has to accept it. I reminded him that you two are the best things that have ever happened to us, since you have allowed us both to be fathers by proxy. And finally I told him that he couldn't blame Clara who didn't ask for anything in this whole matter and that he'd better start loving her like a daughter, which he did during the twenty-four hour wait before the results and the eight and a half months of gestation."

"And what did he answer to that?"

"That he needed to think about it."

I was disappointed. Each of them came to put an arm on my shoulder to comfort me. John commented:

"Well, if I understand correctly, I am the devil by whom misfortune befalls your family."

"Quite the contrary. You'll see in ten years, when the water has flowed under the bridges, I'm sure we'll be laughing about the whole thing," said Paul.

"You're really optimistic!" I exclaimed.

"Yes. Since John came back into my life, I can only be."

They were about to kiss above my head, so I coughed to let them know I was still there.

"I'm going to bed, I'll leave you both."

I left quite confused by what I had just heard. Could Emmanuel give up his silence and his anger to forgive the three of us one day?

CHAPTER 12
THE CHOICE

I hadn't slept all night. Clara neither. She must have felt that I was unwell. If Emmanuel considered my best friend to be the source of all his misfortunes, it was going to be difficult for him to forgive John. But if I had managed it, why couldn't he? And then, what was to become of me without him? I knew in advance that I could never find anyone else for whom I would have such strong feelings. How many times a day did I look at my phone in the vain hope that he would call me? But the call never came.

In the meantime, all the disaster scenarios paraded through my brain. I was lost in guesswork... I thought about how to organize my life without him so as not to feel the pain that his absence was causing me...

Clara started to cry again. It was six in the morning. I took her to bed with me and fell asleep with her on my breast.

Several knocks on the door woke us both. I felt like a minute had passed since I fell asleep. In fact, it was already ten o'clock. Clara had finally let me sleep four hours straight! I was grateful to her.

"Yes?" I asked through the door.

I heard Paul's voice.

"Julia, I'm with Emmanuel."

"What!?"

"Can he come in?"

"Give me a minute."

I looked at myself in the mirror: I was a hot mess. I put

Clara down in her cot, but she began to scream. I spoke to her to calm her down while trying to do my hair and make up quickly. I quickly brushed my teeth and found a pretty sexy silk robe. I hugged Clara, trying to calm her down, and opened the door.

Paul was in front of me and was smiling at me. He took Clara from me, then stepped aside. Behind him appeared Emmanuel. I didn't know if I was still dreaming because his appearance was so unexpected. He was still so handsome but emaciated. He too looked like he hadn't slept all night. Instantly, my heart began to beat faster. I wanted to throw myself in his arms, hug him and never let him go again.

"Hi Julia."

I could still feel his coldness...

"Hi Emmanuel."

"Can I come in?"

"Yes, but it's a mess, sorry."

While waiting to know what fate awaited me, I kept myself busy by opening a window and mechanically making my bed. I was afraid he had come to ask for a divorce.

"Julia, come here."

I walked over to him. He took me in his arms.

"I missed you so much", he said.

It was unexpected and so delicious to rediscover his smell, his arms, his warmth... I whispered:

"You too."

I let myself be overcome by his sadness as he burst into tears. Suddenly he recovered.

"Excuse me, I think it's my nerves."

"You don't have to apologize. I'm your wife until further notice and you have the right to cry in my arms."

"Men don't cry."

Another dumb macho thought! If he remained my husband, I was going to have to set some things straight!

But I wasn't going to get into that debate now that he had finally deigned to speak to me.

He sat down on the bed and motioned for me to join him. Then he lay down and took my hand.

"Julia, the situation overtook me. I felt betrayed. The child we were both expecting is not mine and I resented you and John too. I couldn't believe you don't remember a thing. I'm still struggling with it."

"I talked about it again with John... My memory has still not returned..."

"But hey, it's crazy!"

"Yes, I know. Talk to my brain about it…"

Emmanuel smiled his charming smile that had seduced me from day one. I wanted to kiss him.

"I spoke with my brother yesterday and for the first time since Clara was born, I put myself in your shoes. I realized that I had abandoned you when you needed me most. That I couldn't stay all my life waiting for the pain to pass. I tried to hate you. I even wanted to ask for a divorce. But I can't."

I squeezed his hand in mine, then I started to stroke his arm, his neck… I lingered on his cheek, staring at him, expecting a gesture from him. He took my hand, kissed it, then, unable to contain the distance that separated us, he pulled me to him to kiss me. I felt my whole being revived at his touch. I had missed his skin, his warmth.

This kiss had us on fire and I was hoping that John and Paul weren't waiting for us for breakfast... I didn't know if my body was perfectly ready for what was probably going to happen. I did everything to prevent him from undressing me as I was ashamed of my body... I was afraid Emmanuel would reject me because I had carried a child other than his. But he didn't. When he made love to me, I knew I hadn't lost him...

I felt in my whole being that I was still his soul mate. He stayed in my arms for a long time without speaking.

He was looking at my body transformed by pregnancy. I didn't feel particularly comfortable, but I didn't dare break the spell. I let him watch and reacquaint with me as I did the same. He looked into mine.

"I love you Julia, I never stopped loving you."

"Even when you tried to hate me?"

"I tried, but I never managed to."

I would have liked to ask him a whole bunch of questions, to talk about the future, to know what was going to happen to us according to him, but I preferred to let him talk... We had a little time ahead. I heard Clara scream and footsteps approaching my room. John knocked on the door.

"Are you visible? I think Clara is hungry."

As we were naked, Emmanuel pulled the covers over both of us.

"Get in."

John looked at us dumbfounded when he saw us both in bed, but immediately recovered from his amazement and brought Clara to me.

"I'll leave her with you."

He left as quickly as he had come and closed the door behind him. I put her to my breast. She began to suckle voraciously.

"You were starving", I said.

I stroke Clara's head, then put my hand in Emmanuel's. He didn't push it away. I wanted to tell him that it was also his daughter, that blood ties were not everything. But I had nothing to say, Emmanuel in turn began to stroke Clara's head. Her charm was working on Emmanuel: there was something about that little face that was so cute, so innocent that it was impossible to resist. Well, that's what I thought…

"Julia, I don't know what to do."

"In relation to what?"

"To her."

"What do you mean?"

"What did you decide with John?"

"We didn't decide anything. I was waiting to know if you would come back."

I looked at him. He seemed lost in thought.

"What about you, are you managing to survive with your parents?"

"So far I haven't had a choice."

"You could have gone back to our apartment."

"And risk meeting you there? Or to see the room we had prepared so well for our child deserted? No, I wasn't able to face that."

"And now?"

"Now I think I'm ready to take a step towards you. But I'm not sure I can make it towards Clara yet."

It seemed to me that my heart had stopped. Paul was right. Emmanuel wanted me to abandon my daughter to John. My maternal instinct kicked in and I instinctively pulled Clara closer to me as if he was going to tear her from my arms.

"What do you mean?"

"I don't know, she is not my child, do you understand?"

"Yes, but a lot of children do not genetically descend from their fathers and still call them Daddy. You just have to decide to become one for Clara."

"I don't know if I can. It's beyond my control, I can't help blaming her for being here. I feel like she took away my wife and my fatherhood."

"Emmanuel, if Clara had been our child, she would have stolen the show during breastfeeding anyway. When she is weaned, it will be different. But either way, I couldn't have been entirely yours like before. As for your paternity, I don't know what to tell you about it... You know, I still wish we had children of our own..."

Emmanuel detached himself from me.

"I shouldn't have come. I realize that what I came to ask of you is impossible."

"What did you come to ask me?

"To choose between her and me."

His words caused me such pain that I felt like a dagger had pierced my heart. How could I show him that he could love this child like it was his own?

I began to curse John, calvados and this damned Normandy which had given me a man, certainly, but with such obtuse ideas.

"You can't ask me to abandon Clara."

"I know, and yet this is what I would like."

"But she needs her mother, and I need her. It's like I'm asking you to choose between drawing, which is your job and your passion and me."

He thought for a moment and looked at Clara. Then he began to stroke her head again.

"You see, I don't feel a thing when I do this. Still, I wish I could be like a father to her, but it's as though I'm stuck. I think my hatred of what she represents prevents me from seeing her as anything other than the child I was expecting and never will have. I'm angry at you and John. I know you're going to tell me that you don't remember and that was before you knew me, but I can't control this feeling of rejection towards Clara or even John. I can't hate you either, although it would be much easier. I wish I could tell you that I forgave you and that I am ready to be Clara's adoptive father, but I would be lying to you and I would be lying to myself..."

"What do you suggest then?"

"To leave Clara with John and Paul. That we get back together and have other children. Let's go and live in Paris without her. Like before."

"You want me to abandon my daughter to John and pretend she was never born?"

"I know it sounds crazy, but yes..."

"Then you don't love me Emmanuel."

He looked at me in surprise.

"Of course I do…"

I was so angry and so stunned that I straightened up and got out of bed. I pulled on my dressing gown as best I could while keeping Clara, who was still suckling, in my arms.

"To love is to want the happiness of the other. If you believe that everything can go back to how it was before just by leaving Clara to John, you're kidding yourself. Can you imagine the sadness this will cause me? She's my daughter, Emmanuel, I can't leave her like that! And then do you think I can stay in love with a man who forces me to leave my child? What you ask me would sign our death warrant as a couple. You would be happy, but you would take away a part of me. I can't make that choice. I love you, but abandoning my child is out of the question. At a pinch, I can put up with not seeing her on weekends and leaving her to John half the time so that she can enjoy both her father and her mother alternately if there is no other choice but to abandon her completely? I can't imagine a day without her already…"

I cried in spite of myself. Clara began to scream.

"Don't ask me to choose between you and her. I want you both."

My anger was so bad that I needed to get away from him:

"I'll let you think about it. We'll be downstairs…"

I closed the door on him and the tears streamed down my cheeks. I couldn't believe the love of my life could ask me such a thing. This situation seemed insoluble to me. I wished for one moment that I was dead so as not to be faced with such a difficult choice. If I stayed with him, I would have ended up hating him. But if I chose my daughter, would I hate her for separating me from the man I loved? And was I also going to blame John to whom I had offered this cursed pact?

I left the room, but I didn't want the boys to see me in this state. I locked myself in the bathroom: the one where I had vomited. I looked at these walls and tried to remember. But apart from the stealthy images I had always had, nothing came back.

How could I have felt nothing the next morning? And how could John have been silent, causing this catastrophe eight and a half months later? He had given me the love of my life only to take him back from me... What an irony! Perhaps I was not destined to be happy in love... At the same time, the very idea that Emmanuel might start his life over with another person was unbearable to me. I heard a knock.

"Are you alright?"

I wiped away the tears with my now mascara covered hand and half-opened the door. It was John...

"Do you think I look like I'm ok?"

"No."

"Okay, so don't ask silly questions."

"Let me in, Julia."

"Definitely not! It's your fault that I'm here."

"It's our fault. I'd like to remind you that it is you who asked me to get you pregnant."

I started to cry even more. John was right, it was as much my fault as his. But it was so much easier to hate him rather than myself. Clara was still screaming louder and I pulled myself together to calm her down. I put her back to my breast.

"I don't know what to do. Emmanuel wants me to abandon Clara to go live with him in Paris as if she had never existed. But I could never do that!"

I hugged my daughter while reaffirming her:

"I could never give you up my baby."

"Did he really say that?"

It was Paul who had reacted this time. I heard him

mumble:

"But who does he think he is? Tearing a mother away from her child... He's crazy!"

I didn't want Paul to get involved. I shouted through the door so he could hear me:

"Leave it!"

I wanted to stop him from going up, but Paul had already climbed the stairs four at a time. From below I could hear a heated discussion.

"I think you're wasting your time," said John.

"It won't change anything anyway. Emmanuel is too traumatized by this whole story. He's transfered his hatred to Clara, to you and even to me. Even if we start over as if nothing had happened, it doesn't seem as though it will get better."

"I'm prepared to keep her if that helps. Maybe he just needs some time to get used to the idea?"

"How could he get used to being Clara's stepfather if he never sees her?"

"I don't know, but think about it. I'll deal with her in the meantime if it helps you find your way."

"Impossible! How could I live without her?"

"You'll have to do it anyway if she spends her time between Paris and here. And one day she will go to college and she will have her own life... We have children so that they leave one day. Not for them to stay at home like *Tanguy*."

Emmanuel went down the stairs four at a time followed by Paul, who was yelling at him:

"Where do you think you're going? I'm not finished."

"I need to get out."

"And to run away again? To leave your wife like this?"

Emmanuel gave me a look of anger and despair. Just like the one when he learned the truth.

"I'll send the divorce papers to Paris. You can live in the apartment in the meantime. Don't try to reach me. You made your choice."

"But I have not chosen anything Emmanuel, John was telling me that he was ready to babysit the little one to give us time to find each other again. And maybe you will get used to the idea?"

"What idea? But don't you understand! I could never forgive you. And even less Clara for not being my daughter!"

Emmanuel left, slamming the door. I gave Clara to John and ran after him since I was able to now.

"Emmanuel, I'm begging you!"

I thought I could hold him back, but I should have known better. Just as when he had decided that I was the love of his life the first time he saw me, with a snap of his fingers he had decided that I was no longer worth it. It was his mother who was going to be happy...

CHAPTER 13
SURPRISE!

Since Emmanuel had gone, I had spent my time throwing up. It was great for shedding pregnancy pounds, but not great for breastfeeding. This surprise gastroenteritis kept going.

After a week without any improvement, I was starting to wonder if it was possible that I was pregnant again... But no, it would just be a miracle! I had read that it is extremely rare to get pregnant while breastfeeding.

While going to see my gynaecologist for my check-up, she told me to my great surprise that I was pregnant again! I was going to be able to apply for my place in the Guinness World Records! This time there was no room for doubt. There had been no drunkenness with calva and anyway Paul would have killed me if I had put my hands on his beloved... I began to hope that on hearing the news, Emmanuel would return immediately. As if this baby could make him forget the other...

"It's impossible, I said to the gynaecologist. Are you sure?"

"We're going to take a blood test to check, but I've never been wrong before. In my opinion, you are."

I couldn't believe it: now that I was in the middle of a divorce with the love of my life, I found out that the one time we had sex was enough to get me pregnant! Who had said that the fertility of women over 30 was not so good? Into what kind of trouble had I got myself again?

*

* *

As I was going to resume work the next day, I had left Clara who was now weaned, to John. I had not managed to find a place for her in a nursery. We had therefore decided that it would be less stressful for John to take care of her during the week at Le Tréport and for me to see her on weekends. Leaving her had been heartbreaking. Especially since it was to find myself alone in the apartment that had held so many joys.

I was showing it to potential buyers. The divorce was going to take a while, but I had to find another place to live with Clara.

During the entire time that I had lived in Le Tréport, I had not met Emmanuel since that famous Sunday morning when we had conceived this little being who had started to live inside me without knowing it.

The news of my early pregnancy had given rise to a crazy hope in me: that Emmanuel would change his mind. Maybe knowing that I was pregnant by him, he would finally accept the situation? Maybe also by becoming a father, he would understand the heartbreak it was not to see one's child every day?

Paul had become my only means of communication with Emmanuel. When I left my gynaecologist, I decided to call him. It was lunchtime and I was hoping he would pick up. He answered:

"Salut Julia, to what do I owe the pleasure?"

"I'm leaving my gynaecologist. I just found out that I am pregnant again."

"What?! But who's the father?"

"Your brother, of course!"

"You mean... The day when... But it's crazy!"

"Yes, we can say it is rather unexpected."

"But it's great! I must tell Emmanuel right away! You

always choose the most unlikely times to get pregnant!"

"I know, I know... But I would like to tell him myself and if possible face to face. Do you think we can arrange a meeting with him next weekend at Le Tréport?"

"Maybe you can see him today: he's in Paris for his job."

"Only for the day?"

"Yes. He comes back tonight."

"So I have to show up at his work!"

I looked at myself in the lift mirror and decided to go inside to change and try to find something sexier. It wasn't going to be easy. My stomach had shrunk, yes, but my waist didn't look like it was before I was pregnant. And since I was expecting another child, it wasn't going to get any better. But I saw the bright side: at least I could lose the weight of two pregnancies at once, instead of trying to get back to my original figure after the first, and then have my efforts ruined by a second child.

I prepared as I had for my first date with Emmanuel. I wanted him to feel a pang in his heart when he saw me. If I hurried, I would have time to arrive just before he resumed work. I arrived at 13:58 in front of the entrance to the building.

I saw him walk down the street quickly with a beautiful blonde perched on high heels and strapped into a tight black suit. My opposite. But I didn't have time to dwell on her. Anyway, Emmanuel had a type of girl: me, and she didn't fit that at all. So I didn't feel as though I was in a competition. As soon as he saw me, I saw him say a few short words to his colleague and then rush at me with an angry look.

"What are you doing here?"

"I needed to talk to you."

"Listen, I have no wish to talk to you. I gotta go."

He walked to the door where her colleague was waiting for him. I shouted at him:

"Even if I tell you that I'm pregnant with your child?"

At these words, the colleague quickly slipped away, probably very happy to carry the gossip of the day to the office. Emmanuel retraced his steps.

"What did you just say?"

"I am pregnant with your child. The gynaecologist confirmed it to me."

He frowned incredulously:

"And who tells me it's mine this time?"

"Do you really think I would have invented such a thing?"

"You made me believe that the first child you were expecting was mine."

"Because I was convinced it was yours!"

I didn't want to go back to that argument again...

"Anyway, if you don't believe me, we can do an early paternity test. There will be no possible doubt."

"OK, because this time I will only believe what I see. Listen, I have to go."

Had I told him I had seen a ghost, he wouldn't have reacted with more coldness. My mad hope that he would return on hearing this news had suddenly evaporated. I decided to go immediately to the laboratory next-door:

"Hello. I want to know what the procedure would be to do a paternity test on an unborn child."

"The father should give us a sample of saliva or blood, replied the laboratory assistant. Are you the one who is pregnant?"

"Yes."

"On the other hand for you it will be a little harder: it will be necessary to be able to obtain samples of the chorionic villus obtained by chorionic biopsy between the tenth and the twelfth week of gestation of the baby..."

Great, like I didn't have billions of things to organize and two apartments to visit in the afternoon!

With Emmanuel, we had found on the first visit,

almost exactly our budget and at the limit of the neighbourhood we had chosen and bought it on impulse. Everything seemed so easy with him. Now that I was a single mother, everything seemed more complicated. The apartments I was viewing were rotten. And besides, I had to manage my diary three months in advance with John to arrange the alternating care of Clara. That made a lot of constraints.

If Clara had been Emmanuel's daughter, I would have come home every day to find her and smell her divine baby scent as I hugged her. And above all, I would have fallen asleep in the arms of the man I loved.

I had tried to hate him, but I couldn't either. I put myself in his shoes and understood his point of view: his hurt, his feeling of having been betrayed and even his selfish request to go back to before Clara was born.

I had asked Paul to suggest to Emmanuel that he could get therapy... But apparently he hadn't reacted. Anyway, whenever I had news of my future ex-husband, it was very laidback: "He's fine. He's going out. He's seeing friends again. He's working."

Paul was also going through hell. It was horrible for him in Dijon while he waited to move to Normandy. Besides, Emmanuel had distanced himself from him since he tried to make him listen to reason. Yet they had always been very close in the past. I wondered if Emmanuel had not felt betrayed by his brother now in being a relationship with the person who was my best friend and now the father of my daughter.

As for Audrey, she was angry with Paul and was trying to turn the children against him. She couldn't accept the fact that he was gay, let alone that she was going to be left alone with three children, one of them very young.

I had managed to get an appointment at the last minute at the hospital that evening for Emmanuel so that he could have saliva samples taken and I could meet with an anaesthetist.

Arriving at the hospital early, I asked the secretary where I should go. She showed me the way and I waited patiently for my turn, reading a magazine. As luck would have it, I came across the article: "How can you best manage your divorce?". I read the first paragraph which depressed me. I closed the magazine.

How could Emmanuel doubt that the child was his? I felt that my life would henceforth be filled with voids and absences that were impossible to satisfy. I wished Clara had been there: hugging her was the only thing that gave me comfort in the turmoil. Every time I saw her, I told myself that despite everything, her birth had been worth it. But when she wasn't there, I would go back to thinking that life would have been easier if I had got pregnant at the right time and with the right person from the start. I didn't see what it would change when Emmanuel got the results.

My future ex-husband was still locked in rejection of the situation. He enjoyed it. As though he was the victim and I was the executioner. At the same time, his mother was verbally murdering me at least ten times a day and he still hadn't moved. And then, as soon as he told his story, he was sure to be pitied; "Oh poor husband who had a child that was not his. Nine months for nothing. I would have done the same". A nurse stepped forward:

"Mrs Tellier? Follow me, please."

Emmanuel had not yet arrived. He had not confirmed he would come. Nor did he answer when I called him at 6 p.m. to give him the address and time of the appointment.

Maybe this was his way of getting revenge? To hurt me by not keeping me informed of anything, except by a letter from a lawyer.

An appointment was made the following Saturday to take the sample. The obstetrician explained to me that he would give a local anaesthetic and then take cells through the navel, using a special needle: I was delighted! I was going to have to meet with the anaesthetist immediately.

As I left the office, I saw Emmanuel. He was waiting for his sample to be taken.

"Thank you for coming", I said.

Silence.

"I have to go see the anaesthetist: for me the procedure is a bit more complicated than for you."

"But is there no risk for the child?"

"This potentially increases the risk of miscarriage by 3-5%. You don't seem like you really want to want it anyway, so that doesn't matter, does it?"

"What makes you say that? I'd like to remind you that I'm here."

A little glimmer of hope lit up in my eyes. And then they called me.

"I have to go," I told him. "If you want, I'll meet you right after."

Silence on his part. When I left the anaesthetist's office, there was no sign of Emmanuel. I spent the rest of the evening waiting for a message from him, but the phone remained silent. He had locked himself back in his shell. I couldn't get used to it. I should have turned the page, stopped believing he was coming back, had my famous "white mourning," but the heart of this child that was beating in me kept me from giving up on the love of my life. Clara had separated us, but maybe this baby would allow us to find each other?

I decided to allay the constant stream of my doubts, and simply live in the present moment. Anyway, I was back at work the next day, and I didn't know what to expect after four months away from the office...

I missed my daughter and felt an unworthy mother to be away from her. At the same time, as John had predicted, I was happy to find time for myself away from the crying, and to be able to sleep through the night. I had some sleep to catch up on...

CHAPTER 14
DREAM JOB

Lauren had replaced me during my entire absence. My boss called me a week before I returned to tell me that he needed to speak with me as soon as I arrived at the office. I had only one anxiety: to be pushed aside. Perhaps he had realized that Lauren was doing the job better than me?

For once I was on time. I was even five minutes early, because this interview worried me. I first saw the switchboard operator. She hugged me while answering the phone and gave me the sign that we usually used to let me know that the boss had already arrived. I walked over to my office.

Lauren was not there yet. I breathed, thinking to myself that maybe I could get a five-minute break before my interview without having to put up with her harsh remarks. My boss walked past the open space and saw me settle in. He came towards me with outstretched arms...

"Julia, it's good to see you again!"

"You said that as if you missed me a lot."

"But it's true, I missed you a lot. The office was not the same without you. So how is your daughter?"

"Well. She's in Normandy with her father..."

"Oh really? And how is your husband?"

"I don't know."

"What do you mean?"

"I'll explain it all to you. Shall we have a cup of coffee and start this meeting?"

He bought me coffee from the machine.

"So how have been the last four months?" I asked him.

"Lauren captained the boat pretty well in your absence."

Damn. I could already see myself being pushed aside.

"But that's not what I wanted to talk to you about. You first, tell me a little about the last few months..."

"I don't think you even imagine what a difference it is to have a child."

I told him the main points. Well, except that I was pregnant again. He looked at me dumbfounded.

"You mean you're in the middle of divorce proceedings, that you don't know where you're going to live and that your best friend is keeping your child in Normandy? But it's perfect!"

"What do you mean perfect?"

"Sorry. I mean... A Marketing Manager position has come available. You would continue to do project management but at the brand level. As you are bilingual in English, I know you will be ideal for the job."

"What does English have to do with it?"

"The position is based at the parent company in London. They need someone who speaks French, English and Spanish very well, like you."

"I can tell that you've never heard me speak Spanish... But wait a second, did you say London? You mean I would move there?"

"Yes. Basically you would be based there and you should also go to Spain one day every two months or so."

"Who else knows about it?"

"Lauren doesn't know. I kept the job just for you."

"And when do I have to give you an answer?"

"Before the end of next week if possible."

"That soon?"

"In any case, you are not the only candidate so don't get carried away: there are three. Besides, you have to tell me which days next week I can send you to London."

Having a child part time makes life so much more

complicated. I couldn't go on a whim anymore, I had to calculate everything according to the days I had Clara.

"Uh... Tuesday, Wednesday or Thursday, I replied. But it is imperative that I must be back on Thursday evening. John is coming to drop off my daughter off for the weekend... And in the meantime, what do I do? Is Lauren going back to her old job?"

"We've signed new contracts so having two project managers won't be too many. We will meet later to decide who gets which customers. I asked Lauren to sort your emails. I'll give you two hours to take note of all this and around 11am let's talk about it in the meeting room!"

I found Lauren: her attitude had changed towards me. I don't know if it was because she too had become a project manager by now, but she had not sent a single spade since I arrived. I was waiting for the next arrow still...

At the meeting, I was essentially given back my old clients while Lauren had practically all the new ones. It had been such a busy day that I had only thought of my daughter during the lunch break whereas she had occupied my mind constantly for the past few months. But as I walked out of work, my guilt over leaving her caught up with me.

I called John :

"Hello, all is well with you?"

"Yeah, I was going to finish an email and take Clara for a walk on the beach."

"In this cold?"

"Don't worry, I'll cover her up well and then it won't be for long. She hasn't been out all day. You wouldn't want to deprive our daughter of the good sea air, would you?"

"Obviously not. How is she?"

"Great. I think the nanny takes care of her very well."

"I would love to be there with you."

"Don't worry, you will be soon, it's coming to the end of the week. Hey, what are you waiting for to tell me that you are pregnant again?"

"Sorry, I wanted to tell you about it, but I slept like a log yesterday. Emmanuel didn't believe me when I told him it was his."

"It's a bit normal for him to be on the defensive."

"I don't understand. He knows very well that he's the only man I have been with for a year."

"Yes, but the first pregnancy has completely undermined his confidence in you."

"So, I know you had planned to return to Le Tréport for the weekend. But do you think you could stay until Saturday morning to babysit Clara while I take the test? Otherwise, I'll ask my mother..."

"I'll check with Paul. He's arriving on Friday night, but I could tell him to stay with his parents so that we can meet again on Saturday afternoon. It will make him so happy!"

"I don't want to bother you too much... I'm sure my mother will be happy to babysit Clara otherwise... And shit, that means I'm going to have to tell her I'm pregnant again. And this time, the kid won't even have a father. What if Emmanuel asks me to have an abortion?"

"Do you really think he's going to do that when he wanted this child so badly?"

"I don't know, he hasn't given me any news since I saw him in the hospital yesterday and in my opinion I won't have any until next week with the results of the paternity test... And then my boss offered me a new job."

"What already? As soon as you returned?"

"Yes, he wants me to be a Marketing Manager in London."

"What?! And what did you say to him?"

"That I would think about it…"

I heard silence at the end of the line.

"Are you still there?" I said.

"Yes, sorry, I was thinking... You should accept."

"But are you crazy? What about you and Clara? It's already hard not to see you, if I'm in London it's going to be even worse."

"But on the contrary, think about it... It's only one hour's travel between London and Calais while from Paris it is 1h30. So the Eurostar may be quicker."

"It's true, I hadn't thought about that. What about Emmanuel?"

"Even if he comes back with you, he can work anywhere he wants. He won't be far either if he needs to return to Paris."

"But I'm pregnant. I'm not going to say yes, go there and then quit the job right after."

"Why not?"

"I don't know. Right now I have to go for an interview there. It's not certain I'll get the job."

"And Emmanuel, what has he said?"

"I haven't spoken to him yet. He would have to break his silence."

"You'll see what he tells you. For me, that won't change much except that I'll have to make arrangements to make the round trips to Paris during the day. I will avoid staying for two days. Or I'll go and sleep at my parents', which makes me very happy..."

"I thought things were going better between you guys since you became a dad."

"Yes, when Clara is there. But as soon as they see Paul, it's a bit like Marie-Bénédicte with you and Emmanuel. They can't help but hold him responsible for my perdition."

"I'm coming home, I'll call you back. Give Clara a kiss for me in the meantime."

"I will."

Not being able to speak to her, I couldn't wait to see her through the screen and hear her babble. I missed her. I was afraid she would feel left out. I felt myself to be a completely unworthy mother. But again, I had to make a choice when I had just regained my balance even though it was still precarious.

Should I tell them at the interview that I was pregnant until I knew if her father wanted me to keep the child? What if Emmanuel hated me now so much that he asked me to have an abortion? I couldn't imagine this from my favourite Catholic. I hoped he would instead see the arrival of a new child as a divine sign that he had to come back... If only!

John was kind enough to stay so I didn't have to inform my mother during the operation on Saturday morning to collect the sample. Paul was not exactly thrilled, but during his stay with his parents I had once again given him the task of convincing Emmanuel to come back.

When John left at the beginning of the afternoon for Normandy, leaving me alone with Clara, I was surprised to receive a phone call from Emmanuel. I decided to let him talk and listen to him:

"I just had a conversation with Paul", I said.

"Ah..."

"Did the sampling procedure go well?"

"Yes, we should have the results on Tuesday or Wednesday. I asked that they be sent to your parents and to us so that you will receive them at the same time as me."

Silence on the phone. I was silent too.

"Julia?"

"Yes."

"No nothing. I will be in Paris next Wednesday, if you want I'll come see you at our place after work to talk about the result."

I wondered what this phone call meant. Emmanuel had not called me voluntarily since Clara's birth. Unfortunately, my interview in London was also scheduled for the following Wednesday. I was hoping that Emmanuel would wait for me until I got home. This time, no alcoholic amnesia could make me doubt that he was the father and I hoped he would have the decency to stay home and talk about it.

As I had Clara on my hands, I had little time over the weekend to prepare for my interview. I hadn't done one in years, let alone in English. So I spent hours searching the internet for trick questions that might be asked of me.

Wednesday morning I was on the lookout for the letter with the results, but it was still too early for the mail.

I was very excited to take Eurostar. It had been a long time since I had been to London. I had always loved this city. It vibrated with a special energy, so different from Paris. It always seemed to be on the move. And above all, everyone spoke English...

I had never been to the premises of the parent company. Situated on the bank of the Thames, it had stunning views of Hammersmith Bridge, which, with its few late joggers, contrasted in its calmness with the hustle and bustle of the surrounding neighbourhood. I loved the change of scenery and felt intoxicated by this place...

I was made to wait outside John Pearce's office. I had seen his picture and he looked quite a handsome man on our intranet although a little old to me. But in the flesh, this man was charm embodied. His wide smile when he squeezed my hand confused me. It was the first time that a man other than Emmanuel had made an impression on me since he entered my life.

He had been surprised by my New York accent. Probably less by my Spanish, but he didn't seem to speak it divinely either. I was taking notes so that I wouldn't have to meet his gaze. Yet he did not have the obvious beauty of Emmanuel. His charm came more from his smile.

I had apparently managed to thwart his trick questions.

Towards the end of the interview, he broached the personal aspect.

"Would you be prepared to live in London and go once every two months to Spain?"

"Yes. Absolutely."

"What does your family say about it?"

"They've told me not to miss out on this opportunity in my career."

"Alright, I think I have no more questions. Do you have any for me?"

"Yes, if I was offered the job, when would I start?"

"Next Monday."

"That fast?"

"Yes, but we would provide you with a staff apartment. We are already very behind recruiting for this role and we really need someone ASAP."

"And when will you give me your answer?"

"Friday morning."

"So if you take me, I will have to move... This weekend?"

"Yes. Did you have something planned?"

"No, nothing that can't be reorganised."

I was thinking of my daughter. The idea that next Monday I could work there worried and relieved me all at the same time. Sure, it would be a huge stress to move in a weekend but maybe, by starting a new life elsewhere, the ghosts of the past would haunt me less. In fact, this idea was ridiculous: I carried within me the child of my past. Would he or she be part of my future? I didn't have a clue.

Besides, I didn't know if Emmanuel would be expecting me tonight. I wanted to say goodbye to my charming and possible future boss, but he told me he would join us for lunch with my colleagues.

It was a test, I was sure. All nine members of the team were there. Three of my direct contacts, John Pearce and five other people. I wondered if they had lunched like this with all the candidates or if it was a special treat for me who was already in the seraglio. It corresponded to their monthly meal with colleagues.

It was cold that day in March, but there was a wonderful winter sun on the banks of the Thames. We all sat outside under heaters and blankets with fish and chips. I found the whole team very nice and this lunch was all jokes and questions about life in France.

I was the centre of attention and was afraid to say something that might work against me. I didn't see the clock ticking and realized with horror that I was going to miss my Eurostar if I didn't hurry. So I left them and hurried back to Hammersmith on foot. Luckily the Piccadilly Line took me directly to Saint Pancras.

Once in the Eurostar I kept thinking about Emmanuel... Would he agree to come back to me with the confirmation that I was carrying his child? Could he bear that Clara and John were inevitably part of my life? Would he come with me if I asked him to go to London?

This city seemed like the ideal escape to me now. I would no longer have to live in our apartment and would save money for six months by living on expenses. Just the time of my pregnancy. I could then go and give birth in Normandy and take extended maternity leave if I wanted to. It wouldn't be very cool for my employer, but for me it would be the only way to see my two kids together and watch them grow up for a year or two.

I could never have an abortion, I knew that. I had waited so much for Emmanuel's child... I wrote him a text message to let him know of my arrival.

Emmanuel did not answer, as usual. But imagine my surprise when I saw that he had come to meet me at the Gare du Nord.

How to react? Jump on his neck, give him a kiss or stay away? I hadn't touched him since the day he unknowingly got me pregnant, then rejected me so violently. As I approached, I saw that he was holding a letter in his hand. He must have come to our house to get the results... He handed it to me before I could take a step closer to him. I opened it and saw what I already knew.

"We need to talk", he said.

"I know. Do you want to go home?"

"No, I'm taking you to the restaurant."

I didn't know if it was a good thing or a bad thing. The restaurant was a neutral place where I couldn't make a scene. Emmanuel didn't say a word the whole way there. Much to my surprise he took me to where it all began: *Aux pieds dans l'eau*.

The terrace was closed at this time of year. It was still too cold to dine outside. It was almost a shame to come here without being able to enjoy it. And to think that we would have celebrated our anniversary here in a month. Why had he brought me here? If it all started there, everything could also end there.

The waiter placed us at an isolated table. There weren't many people there that night. Emmanuel still said nothing. He was studying the menu. It looked like he was waiting... Maybe for the right time? I ordered the same as when we first came with the only difference that there was no wine this time around. When the waiter was finally gone, Emmanuel took my hand to my astonishment. He saw that I was still wearing my wedding ring.

"You kept it?" he said.

"Yes. I'm still your wife until further notice."

He stared at me thoughtfully.

"Look, I ... I'm a little stunned by this news. I was not expecting that at all."

"Me neither, but if you'll allow me, I think that's a sign."

"A sign?"

"Yes, the sign that we must not separate so that we can raise this child together."

"I no longer know Julia. So much has happened since our first night here..."

I played my all-out.

"You know, I think our future comes down to one question: do you still love me?"

"And you, do you still love me?"

"I've never stopped loving you and hoping that you come back."

"Ah..."

He was silent for a moment and his gaze moved to the part of the terrace, where we had kissed for the first time.

"What were you doing in London today?"

"I had an interview."

He opened his eyes wide. I explained to him:

"My company would like to send someone there. If they pick me, I'll find out on Friday and will have to move over the weekend; I will have a staff apartment for six months while I find something else."

"And are you going to go if you get the job?"

"London-Calais-Le Tréport or Paris-Calais-Le Tréport, is practically the same. I will only see Clara on weekends and at least I will be able to vacate our apartment faster. John agrees, he told me to take the job."

"What about me in all of this? What about our child?"

"You have to tell me if you want a future with us."

I put my hand on my stomach. The waiter arrived at that moment with our dishes. I had no more appetite. I just wanted one thing, for him to tell me whether or not he wanted to get back with me. If it were to hurt, I'd rather be done, and soon.

"When you told me you were pregnant with our child, I thought you had made up this story to get me back..."

"You know I'm not a manipulator."

"I know I know. Or rather, I don't know anything anymore. The birth of Clara changed everything in my head. I lost confidence. In you, in John, in life. I hated

Clara, hated you for creating this child almost behind my back."

I calmly told him again what he knew.

"Emmanuel, I didn't know you when John and I conceived Clara accidentally. I still don't remember sleeping with him and if I had remembered I would have told you immediately. I don't know how to apologize or ease your pain or your feeling of betrayal. I wish I could erase what happened, but I can't. With you, Clara is the best gift life has given me. And I'm overjoyed to know that I'm pregnant with your child again. I'm just afraid you'll ask me to have an abortion..."

"I will never ask you for such a thing! I too have always dreamt of having a baby with you."

Phew. It had been my biggest fear.

"You told me you tried, but failed to hate me. So I ask you the question again. Do you still love me?"

"I think I do."

I smiled shyly, but he looked away.

"So what is it?"

"I'm afraid I won't be able to love Clara and forgive you."

"Emmanuel, I don't want you to take it the wrong way, but during all this time that we were apart, did you seek help… the psychological sort?"

"No."

"Why?"

"Because I prefer to face this situation alone."

"And did you overcome it?"

"I don't know. I just went through the most horrible months of my life without you."

"Me too."

"So, are you going to go to London on your own?"

"I never said that. I don't even know if I'm going to get the job yet, I'm just saying it's a possibility and if you wanted to you could come with me. We could start a new life... You and me in a new town where no one knows us."

"I don't know, I feel good in Normandy and my job has asked me to come back to Paris one day a week."

"I won't do anything that could compromise a possible future for you and me. If you tell me that you want to live in Le Tréport, I'll come with you. I will find another position in a nearby town. Never mind."

"You would do that for me?"

"Yes, of course."

"And you don't hate me for abandoning you?"

Yes. To death. But if you come back, I'm ready to forgive you for everything.

"I could never hate you..."

Emmanuel looked at me and took my hand.

"I missed you."

"I missed you too…"

CHAPTER 15
LONDON

I had accepted the position... Emmanuel had given us a second chance. We would go back to Normandy every weekend as long as my pregnancy allowed. Then John would bring Clara to London for the last time until my maternity leave.

In the meantime, we had kept the Paris apartment so that Emmanuel could stay there when he had to go to work. As the London apartment was furnished, we didn't have so much to move, so we only took clothes. Either way, we wouldn't have had the space or time to take more in the Eurostar.

I had the impression that Emmanuel and I were living again the ecstasy of the beginnings. It was as if we were trying to make up for lost time. We spent our evenings in each other's arms... Emmanuel had started doing psych sessions via Skype. I felt it helped him a lot to cope with the situation, even though he never told me about it...

I had spent the last weekend alone at Le Tréport with Clara and John. He had asked me for a little time before he felt ready to see her again.

I had only one fear, and that was that he might not be able to overcome his feelings of aversion when he saw her.

In any case, for the moment, I felt alive again. However, I had to learn a lot of things for my new job and the pregnancy was tiring me. But the excitement of being in London and starting to live together again prevailed...

I hadn't told anyone I was pregnant. No one could see

it at the moment. I wasn't sure how or when to announce it... I thought I'd say it in a month's time when I had proven myself a bit. Either way, it would show. I was not very proud not to have said anything at the interview, but I would have done anything to stop working with Lauren because after the first days of calm after my return, she had started to be hateful again.

Emmanuel had already left for Paris the day before and I was to meet him directly in France on Friday evening. I arrived after him because of the time difference. He picked me up at Calais station.

My visceral urge to touch him had increased because of the months without him. I felt that he too needed to hug me and we stood there for a long time, kissing each other on the platform like two lovers thirsty for each other.

When I got there, I couldn't help but go to see my daughter sleeping. Was I ever going to get used to living away from her?

It had been barely two weeks since I had started working again, but it already seemed like an eternity from the months I had taken care of Clara day and night. She had grown again this week and I was angry that I hadn't been there to see it. Clara coughed lightly. I covered her so she wasn't cold. Then I kissed her gently without waking her and I returned to the living room where John, Emmanuel and Paul were having a drink. I was moved to see them reunited. Paul saw me arrive:

"Ah, there you are, Julia! My father called earlier. He wants to invite us all to lunch on Sunday."

"John too?" asked Emmanuel.

I had completely forgotten that coming back with my husband while Paul was John's companion meant that I was also going to have to see the Mother Superior again. I really hadn't missed her at all.

"Yes, John is invited", said Paul.

"But it's the revolution !" I said.

I came to curl up in Emmanuel's arms on the sofa, but he withdrew his arm. Ouch. I hoped he wasn't changing his mind. John handed me an herbal tea. We were far from calva. Well, being a mother makes you wiser!

"But that means they're ready to accept that you are gay?" I said.

"I think so. My father told Mum that he had been on the brink of death, that he wasn't even sure he was out of the woods and that he didn't want to live the rest of his life in conflict or without seeing his children and grandchildren."

"And what did your mother say to that?" I asked.

"Apparently nothing. She sulks," says Paul.

"Well, that's promising!" I whispered.

Emmanuel stood up suddenly:

"I'm going to bed."

I knew it was better not to insist. Maybe Emmanuel was having a bad time that his father had accepted the situation when he himself had not yet done so? Or was it seeing John again and being in the house that sheltered Clara?

When I came to join him in bed, he was sleeping. Was he pretending? I hugged him, but he shrugged his shoulders to get rid of me. I turned to the other side. Knowing him, there was no point in trying once more. I hoped he would sleep on it.

When Clara woke me up at five in the morning, I didn't dare bring her back to bed with us. She fell asleep again after I gave her a bottle. I had to get up around 8am to take care of her, but no trace of Emmanuel until 11am when he finally deigned to get out of bed and take a shower.

"Do you want to eat?" I asked him.

"No thanks."

He hid in our room until it was time to go to his parents. He hadn't said hello to Clara and hadn't even neared her pram on the journey to get there.

As I rang the doorbell of this house where I had not set foot for months, I was apprehensive. I knew Emmanuel's parents knew about everything that had happened. It was therefore astonished when Barthélémy, emaciated and transformed by illness, hugged me tightly.

"But you hid from me that my granddaughter was so beautiful!"

In one sentence he had done what Emmanuel had not yet managed to do: consider her as part of the family despite her at least indirect parentage... I loved Barthélémy all the more. If only Marie-Bénédicte could do the same... Barthélémy gave her back to me after having kissed her. Clara had reacted rather well to the contact with her grandfather by proxy...

But she began to cough again into my arms as she had done in the night, then all morning. This cough was starting to worry me seriously. Her coughing fits were getting closer and closer. Barthélémy took John in his arms.

"John Langlois... It's been years since we last saw you here!"

But what had got into Emmanuel's father? Even John was stunned by this welcome. Thinking about it, it didn't surprise me that much. Barthélémy seemed to me to be a good man, but one who had allowed himself to be influenced a little too much by his wife. Close to death, it seemed as though he had managed to assert himself towards her.

"Where is Marie-Bénédicte?"

"She's coming. She went to buy some bread."

"Ah... And you Barthélémy, how are you feeling?"

"Better, but still weak. This treatment has completely taken all strength out of me. But these are old men's stories... Tell me instead how your move to London went..."

"Well, the apartment was waiting for us already furnished. So we just brought suitcases of clothes."

"That's convenient. And you John, what have you been doing all these years?"

"I lived and studied in Paris and now I am a Marketing Director in the same company as Emmanuel."

"So you are the reason why I get to see my two sons more often. I thank you!"

John did not know what to answer as he wasn't expecting so much gratitude. The Mother Superior made her entrance at this moment.

"Ah, but you've all already arrived!"

She held out her hand to John, then gave me an icy kiss before kissing her two sons effusively. Paul was holding Clara in his arms and as soon as Marie-Bénédicte saw her, she began to smile at her. Clara began to cry. Obviously, she wasn't her mother's daughter for nothing! Barthélémy commented:

"Marie-Bénédicte has always adored babies, she can't resist them…"

And indeed, I felt like I was dealing with a whole different person. She was beaming with joy… I understood better why she had had four children…

"But how cute she is! How old is she now?"

"Three months."

She took Clara in her arms and tried to stop her crying, without much success. John took her in turn and her coughing fit redoubled. He looked to see if she had soiled her nappy. I took my daughter from her father's arms and asked Emmanuel to come with me to help me change her.

He wasn't going to get away with trying to hide. I was trying to get him used to his "adopted" daughter. Maybe by making him do things with her, he would one day come to love her instead of hating her in spite of himself.

He took me to the upstairs bathroom and I asked him to undo Clara's Babygro. He sighed. It was as though he was afraid to touch her. As he was undressing her, I was shocked: Clara started to gasp and couldn't breathe. I felt with horror as I put my hand to her forehead that it was burning hot. I asked Emmanuel:

"Do you know a doctor at Le Tréport?"

"Yes, but on a Sunday lunchtime I'm not sure if he is available."

"I'm begging you, go find his number and call him. Quickly!"

He finally understood the emergency. He rushed up the stairs and I heard Marie-Bénédicte and John came up immediately.

"What's wrong with her?"

"She can't breathe and has a fever."

John took her in his arms and put his hand on her forehead.

"She's hot..."

Emmanuel rushed back up.

"I can't reach the doctor. We need to get her to the hospital right away."

Clara was getting redder and redder as I dressed her.

"Everything will be fine sweetheart, we'll go see what you got," I said to calm her down.

But my instinct as a mother told me it was serious and I panicked completely. Emmanuel must have felt my mad anguish. He whispered to me:

"Don't worry. We're fifteen minutes from the hospital, I'm going to go start the car and call 999 to let them know we're coming."

I hurried to finish dressing Clara, then John took her in his arms.

We all left together except the grandparents. For the first time, I felt that Clara really had three dads. We were a family –odd of course– but a family all the same. We only thought about the survival of this little being...

At the hospital, Clara didn't have to wait long. The

doctor took her to a room and inspected her tongue. Then he made us unbutton her clothes to listen to her chest. Finally, he took a breathing machine and placed a mask over Clara's mouth.

"But what does she have?"

"I think she has laryngitis. Don't worry, it's very frightening to see in a baby, but there's nothing to be afraid of. She's a tiny being, so when her larynx thickens she seems like she has no more air to breathe. It's okay, I'll give her antibiotics, we'll leave her on an artificial respirator for another quarter of an hour. The hardest part is over."

It was unbearable to watch her chest inflate and then deflate with the machine. I was so scared of losing her... I held her hand and stared into her eyes frightened by the noise. John was holding her other hand, while Emmanuel stroked her forehead.

From that point on, I knew Emmanuel would never see Clara as an enemy again. I hoped that he had finally understood that it had nothing to do with it, that she was the result of a moment of distraction, and that she only wanted a little love in this world...

*
* *

It was very difficult for me to leave my daughter to get back to London that evening. Even though John told me he would take good care of her, I couldn't help but think that I was leaving her when she was still sick and needed me.

On the way back, I did not speak. I just looked at the pictures of Clara on my phone... Every time I left her in the weeks that followed, my heart sank. Yes, I was delighted to have reunited with Emmanuel and to have time for us, but I missed Clara.

I only dreamed of one thing, living with him and her, without having to say goodbye to Clara every week. She always cried when I left and it was heartbreaking for me. Yet John tried to reassure me by telling me that two minutes after my departure she was laughing as if nothing had happened.

My mother used to tell me that I was crazy: according to her, any parent would dream of being in my place so that they could sleep instead of being woken up by their offspring crying at all hours of the night.

My belly started to indicate that it was time for me to tell my colleagues that I was pregnant... Everyone was surprised, but I got nothing but congratulations. It would have been completely different in France. Not a single look askance, although I had only recently joined the company headquarters. Surprisingly, my boss just asked me if he should plan a short leave or a long leave. I told him I had to think about it a bit more.

In truth, my mind was made up. I absolutely wanted it to be long so that I could be with Clara every day during the last months of my pregnancy. Above all, I wanted us to be able to live in Normandy with John, Emmanuel and the children for at least a year.

I was starting to tell myself that my career was much less important to me than my little ones and I was hoping that this year of reflection would give me some time to find an alternative to the situation. Maybe after all, I'll be able to find a job near Le Tréport? I had never really looked for one. We had not yet raised the subject with either Emmanuel or John and I admit that I had postponed the moment of this conversation so much I thought it would not enchant either of them.

From now on, we would go instead to stay with Emmanuel's parents on weekends to leave John and Paul alone. They had even more time to catch up than we did!

Especially since Marie-Bénédicte was pleasant towards Clara even though she forgot to behave the same with me. And I was ready to accept it now that everything was more or less back in order in my life. We even thought of renting something halfway between the two houses to be autonomous.

Emmanuel was almost back to before Clara was born. As considerate as when I was pregnant with Clara. It was I who had changed. The fact that I didn't lose my shape and got pregnant again right away hadn't helped me much to regain any feelings of seductiveness. Even though Emmanuel assured me that I was still as beautiful to him as ever, I found it hard to believe him. Above all, I now found all kinds of excuses to hide myself when it came to making love which had never occurred to me before. One night when he was trying to undress me he stopped dead and told me he was coming back. Five minutes later, he took me by the hand.

I followed him. He had run a bath for me. There was moss everywhere and he had lit little candles. He closed the door then turned off the light. The half-light made it much easier for me to let myself take my clothes off. I tried to undress Emmanuel too.

"No, this bath is for you…"

I looked at him questioningly, but he led me over to the bath and helped me into it. Then he told me to close my eyes and I felt him massage my shoulders and temples. Finally, he caressed me from head to toe. Unable to take it any longer, I undressed him and this time he let me do so. I made him come into the tub, forgetting all about my pregnant woman reserve. From that night on, I stopped being afraid.

As for Emmanuel, I saw him becoming more and more attached to Clara. Since her laryngitis, he had finally started to help me with everything about her when we were with her. Seeing his parents delighted as soon as we arrived and treating her as though she was their granddaughter did a lot, I think, to be a game-changer. In particular, Barthélémy kept telling him how having children was a blessing.

One evening when the four of us were having dinner together after having put Clara to bed, Barthélémy told us that his wife had lost their first child at birth.

I understood from this revelation why Marie-Bénédicte had given up everything to raise her children afterwards.

"Life is precious and we have only one," he said to us.

I looked at my belly and said a little prayer that all would be well for my unborn child. I didn't know if we could overcome another ordeal with Emmanuel. The separation from Clara was getting more and more difficult.

My boss was extremely understanding when I finally told him that I would be taking a long leave.

Fatigue from work, cumulative commuting, and the stress of finding a home caused me to have contractions by the sixth month. My doctor was worried and aware of my situation decided to get me to stop much sooner than expected. He told me to stay in bed as much as possible during the day to prevent the baby from being born prematurely.

I said goodbye to London with relief. It was in the week I got home that we finally found the home we needed. It was three minutes' walk from John's place door to door. If all went well, we could move in before our child was born.

The pregnancy went well until the day of the move. The stress surely made my waters break a week before the due date. This time, Emmanuel was there: he had taken a week off to carry out the move since I couldn't do anything. I left Clara with John who was helping us that day and we went off to the hospital. The same one where we had urgently taken our daughter a few months earlier.

Clara had taken barely three hours to arrive. For my second child, the nurses had barely put me straight on the delivery area when they saw that the head was already sticking out. I was never able to lie on my back and had to stay in that position to give birth. Emmanuel supported me throughout. Twenty minutes later, I was holding our son against my breast. I recognized Emmanuel in his face: they looked so much alike.

I started to cry with joy. I couldn't believe that despite all these hardships, Emmanuel and I were still together and that we had finally given birth to our first child. I was the one who insisted on giving him the first name Victor. It seemed to me that it suited our son well, who would inevitably be victorious because he had managed to get his parents back together when all else had failed.

The first days with our son were wonderful compared to those of Clara. Emmanuel was mad with happiness. He had called the whole family, taken tons of photos and sent tons of emails. He adored his son.

As for Clara, she had come to see her brother from the first day with John, but she was still too small and did not yet realise she had a brother. However, she smiled at him when she saw him, and I took that as a good omen.

John took a picture of the four of us and it was the first picture that was hung in our new house. Poor John had supervised our move while looking after Clara... He was worn out!

The first few weeks were complicated, time to secure everything for Clara and Victor and especially to get used to babysitting two children during the day. It was a really good thing to have two dads in the end: I was happy when John took over taking care of Clara while Emmanuel took care of Victor after work.

But what would happen after this year off? I thought about it sometimes and thought to myself that maybe it would be easier to separate myself from my children. Still, I wanted too much to see them grow. The days had passed too quickly since the birth of Clara, then that of Victor.

I would ask myself the question later... I had wanted these children too much not to see them grow up. Sometimes, living between two houses and two dads against a backdrop of sibling jealousy made things a little more complicated. But for nothing in the world I would have compromised the balance we had created for our children, at least for now.

I hoped that the future would provide a solution for me to maintain this temporary arrangement, and turn it into something lasting... But that was without counting on what awaited me...

TABLE OF CONTENTS

PREGNANT AT ANY COST!

1. THE CLOCK IS TICKING……………..…………….....................9
2. ONE GLASS TOO MANY……………..……………...................13
3. EMMANUEL……………..…………...25
4. A MONDAY LIKE NO OTHER……………..……………...........37
5. AT LAST!……………..…………..57
6. THE PARENTS' ORDEAL……………..…………......................65
7. SEVEN MONTHS AND A HALF WITHOUT CLOUDS…….91
8. JUST A LITTLE DETAIL……………..……………....................97
9. END OF AMNESIA……………..………….............................109
10. THE TRUTH BENEATH THE VERNIX……………..……....127
11. BABY BLUES……………..…………......................................145
12. THE CHOICE……………..…………......................................161
13. SURPRISE!……………..…………..171
14. DREAM JOB……………..…………..179
15. LONDON……………..…………..193

A HUGE THANK YOU

This book would have never seen the light day had my friend Thomas not given me the idea without meaning to. So I thank him!

Thanks to H.B O'Neill, my writing partner in crime for his acute advice and his help in structuring the plot as well as to Lætitia and especially Federica for their help.

Thanks to Alexia, Justine and Lucia for the tales of when they gave birth. Thank you to my proofreaders for their sound advice and the precise tracking of mistakes: Alexis, Anaïs, Christine, Coralie, Federica, Françoise, Geneviève, Jacqueline, Jérémie, Lucia, Marianne, my father, Thomas, Lætitia, Vanessa and especially Catherine for the English version. And to Lily Guillard for her advice.

A special thanks to my publisher who helped me give birth at the same time painfully and exquisitely of this final version that you have in your hands.

Thanks at last to you my reader who has finished this book! I hope you had a great time reading it. If you liked it, don't hesitate to recommend it to your friends and to write me a comment on my Facebook page:

http://www.facebook.com/julialaserie

© June Caravel 2021
Printed by BOD
November 2021